Summer Heat

By Scott Fields

Outer Banks Publishing Group
Outer Banks • Raleigh

Cover design by
Gary Val Tenuta
GVT Grafix
GVTgrafix@aol.com

FIRST EDITION
eISBN 13 – 978-1-4524995-5-0
ISBN 10 - 0982993110
ISBN 13 – 978-0-9829931-1-8

May 2012

Chapter One

Sunlight poured through the dusty window sending ghostlike shadows onto the floor. A gentle breeze sent soft curtains swaying hypnotically back and forth. Somewhere outside, the mournful sounds of cicadas drifted across the morning air. A young woman lay naked on the bed, the sheets pulled back and half-lying on the floor. Beads of sweat trickled across her moist body spilling over her side and disappearing into the already soaked bed.

It was the second year of a drought that had turned the once lush and fertile farmlands of that part of the country into a barren wasteland. Clouds of dust swirled across the vast fields of bull thistle and ragweed. Deep fissures snaked, aimlessly, across the concrete-like earth giving it an eerie, almost unearthly appearance.

Rusted springs screeched as the young woman swung her legs around and sat on the edge of the bed. It had been a long night, a long restless night. She couldn't remember the last time she had slept the entire night. She ran her fingers through her long blond hair. It was soaked with sweat but felt good in the soft breeze from the open window.

She got to her feet and walked slowly over to the window. The breeze felt good on her bare stomach. She lifted the window as far as it would go. The warm morning air cooled as it caressed her sweaty body. She arched her back and stretched waking her tired muscles to another day.

Jessie peered out the window, across the barren front lawn to the dirt road that ran in front of their farm. She smiled. An older pickup truck was stopped in the road, its motor idling as if it were ready to leap forward at a moment's notice. More than likely it was teenage boys. Wasn't the first time. Seemed like they were always out there snooping around, hoping to see something. Good thing for them Frank didn't see them. He'd surely take a shotgun after them. She turned slowly around to give them the full view, then disappeared from sight. Tires spun sending gravel flying in the air.

The cold shower felt good. It seemed to refresh, almost nourish her. She turned slowly under the showerhead letting the cold water splash over her body until goose bumps appeared. She stepped out of the shower, and, without drying herself with a towel, slipped on a pair of frayed denim shorts and a man's tee shirt. She walked down the hallway to the kitchen leaving wet footprints behind.

"Morning, Frank," she muttered, her soaked shirt now clinging to her body.

"Fresh coffee on the stove," he said staring at her chest. "Where's your bra?"

Jessie poured herself a cup of coffee and sat at the table. "It's too hot to wear it," she said lighting a cigarette. "Besides, who's going to see me?"

"Porter will be getting up soon," said Frank sipping his coffee.

"So, I'm his step mom."

"He's also twenty years old."

"What's that supposed to mean?"

"You know very well what it means."

Jessie paused. "It really doesn't matter much. He don't ever get up 'til the afternoon, and I'll be long gone."

"You still going through with it?"

"I start this afternoon."

"Back at the diner?"

She nodded her head.

"I don't want you going back there."

Jessie set her cigarette in an ashtray and sipped her coffee. "It's the only job in town. Besides, we need the money."

"Don't like it," he muttered. "Don't like it at all."

Frank was a big man, nearly six and a half feet tall. It had been said and argued by many of the residents of the small town of Steam Corners that Frank had never smiled or laughed, a stark contrast to his wife, Jessie, who, by most accounts was the party girl of the county. He was forty-four years of age, and the twelve-year difference between he and his wife was another source of gossip in town.

Frank was the son of Porter Harlan Sr., the richest and, considered by many, to be the most successful farmer in the county. When Porter died, he left his money to his grandson, who was named for him, and the ranch to Frank, his only son. Frank struggled to make a living from the farm even before the drought. Then, with no viable source of income, Frank was forced to sell off parcels of the ranch just to stay out of bankruptcy.

For the first time in their five-year marriage, Frank was leaving home. He was offered a job over in Jefferson County, and even though he would be gone for two months, he knew he had to take it.

"When are you leaving?" asked Jessie snubbing out her cigarette.

"Pretty quick."

Jessie looked over her shoulder. There were two large bags by the door. "Wish you didn't have to go."

Frank picked up dirty dishes from the night before and slid them in the sink. "Wish you wouldn't lie to me. It's not very becoming."

"I'm not lying," she snapped. "I really don't want you to go."

Theirs was a relationship that was born from an affair that was not only indiscreet but also flagrantly open for public gossip. Frank had been married to Margaret Thew, his childhood sweetheart and nearly perfect match to his own personality. She was born of average looks, gaunt in stature and lacking any feminine charms. Quiet in nature, she rarely said a word or expressed feelings either orally or physically. Frank soon found himself in a comfortable marriage that in time evolved into an unexciting, loveless relationship with no warmth and no sex. A young man in his twenties, Frank was frustrated and felt trapped in a web of despair. Their union did spawn Porter, their only child, but, as Frank later described his sex life with Margaret, Porter was truly an exception to a perfectly sexless marriage.

Jessie worked as a waitress at the diner, and was everything Frank and every other man in Steam Corners dreamed about. She was an unbridled filly who would never be tamed. As a child she learned that big smiles and light-hearted flirtation with men opened doors and got her most anything she desired. It started with her father, who found her to be irresistible and continued with just about every man who walked into her life. It soon became a habit with her. She craved the attention she got by her incredibly flirtatious smile and her captivatingly seductive eyes.

All men became a challenge to her. It was a game with her and getting them to ask her out, smile sheepishly or even blush was the prize to be won. Frank was her ultimate challenge not only because of his quiet nature but his wealth as well.

After a hot and torrid affair, hidden from very few and a sometimes messy and very public divorce, Frank and Jessie were married. They spent the first few months in the bedroom. Frank seemingly could not get enough. Then as the pressures of the farm and everyday problems began to mount, Frank seemed to drift away and became disinterested in Jessie in or out of the bedroom.

Then as the drought dragged on month after month, the pressures of the farm grew into fears as Frank battled to keep it from bankruptcy. He grew distant from Jessie almost a stranger. The only thing they had left in common was the place in which they lived.

Frank sat down across from Jessie. He reached out and took her hand in his.

"I'm scared Jessie," he said staring down at the table.

"Scared of what, Frank?"

"I know in my heart that if you go back to that diner, you're going to find someone else."

She scooted her chair closer and took his hands in hers. "How can you say that, Frank?"

"Let's face it, Jessie; things haven't been that good between us. Can't remember the last time we made love."

"Well, you certainly can't blame…"

"I know what you're thinking, and, for the most part, you're right. Seems like anymore all I think about is the farm. Can't say as I would blame you if you did find someone else."

"I can't believe you're talking like this."

"Well, I know how you are."

Jessie sat straight in her chair. She pulled her hands away. "What do you mean by that?"

"I didn't mean anything at all."

"You're saying I'm sleazy, aren't you?"

"No, I'm not," said Frank. "I'm just saying that you like to flirt, that's all."

"That was before I married you."

"I just worry about you around all those men in that diner."

"Frank, I wouldn't do anything that would hurt our relationship."

"I'd like to believe you."

Jessie smiled. "Hey, you're the one who is leaving. I should be worried about you finding another woman."

"I think you know better than that."

"How long do you think you will be gone?"

"We should have the job done in two months," said Frank. "It's only a hundred miles away. Maybe I can come home for a weekend or two."

Frank got to his feet and set his coffee cup in the sink. "I gotta go," he said turning to her.

Jessie sprang to her feet and buried her head in his chest. Frank wrapped his massive arms around her and held her tight. It had been a long time since he had even held her, even longer since they had made love. It felt good being in his arms. It seemed to awaken something inside her that had been dormant. She held him closer. Standing on her toes, she stretched up to him, her eyes closed, her lips slightly parted. He bent down and kissed her. It was a long passionate kiss, the kind she had almost forgotten. It felt good. She felt something stirring inside her. He never kissed her like that unless he wanted to make love. He must want her. Why else would he do that? She backed away slightly and ran her tongue lightly over his lips. She heard him moan and pull her even closer.

They had started something that seemingly couldn't be stopped. He could feel the wetness from her tee shirt as it soaked through his. He reached for her breast. He felt a tingling in his loins when he felt her hard nipple. At first, he thought it must be because of the cold, wet shirt, and then he remembered that it wasn't while she was sitting down.

"Come on," she whispered. "Let me take care of you before you leave."

As if awakened from a trance, he backed away until he was against the wall. "No, I can't. I'm already late." He turned and started across the room.

Jesse watched him walk away. She took deep breaths to slow her racing heart and heavy breathing. "Sometimes, I don't understand you," she said running her hands through her hair.

Frank picked up his bags and opened the door. "I'm late, Jessie. I gotta go."

"How can you do that?" she snapped. "How can you just up and walk away?"

"I'm leaving now, Jessie. Please don't be mad at me. I don't want to leave here in the first place, and I sure don't want to leave when you're mad at me."

Jessie forced a smile. "I love you, Frank Harlan."

Frank smiled back. "I love you too, Mrs. Harlan."

It was early afternoon when Porter stumbled down the stairs. He was twenty years old, tall and wiry. With his unkempt sandy colored hair and his deep blue eyes, there wasn't a single woman in the county who hadn't seen him in a fantasy...half the married women as well.

Jessie was sitting at the table smoking a cigarette when he entered the room. He was holding his head with both hands as he fell into one of the chairs.

"Damn, woman, what d'ya got for a headache?"

"Maybe if you didn't drink so much, you wouldn't have a hangover everyday," she said snubbing out her cigarette.

"Maybe if you get yer butt up and get me something, I could get rid of it."

Jesse stood and turned to open a kitchen cabinet. She was wearing frayed denim shorts that when she stretched to reach the aspirin bottle on the top shelf revealed the curves of her almond-shaped bottom.

"Good God, girl," he said staring at her backside. "Are you gonna wear that to the diner?"

She turned and set the bottle on the table. She was wearing a silk shirt that was only partially buttoned. I ain't working at the diner. I'm going to work at Coonie's."

"Good Lord, I don't believe it," he said with a smile. "But you told Pop you were going back to the diner."

"There's no way he would have let me work in a bar," she said sitting back down.

"So why are you doing it?"

"Bigger tips," she said. "We need the money."

"You know what that means?" he shouted.

She sensed it was a rhetorical question and didn't reply.

"It means free beer for me."

"Don't even think about it. Besides, I won't ever wait on you."

"Why's that, darlin'?"

"Like I said before, I want big tips."

Porter opened the aspirin bottle and shook a few into his open hand. He picked up a glass from the table that had orange juice from breakfast.

"I don't know," he said gulping down the pills. "They tell me I'm quite the tipper when I get hammered."

"Which is every night," said Jessie. "Besides, it just don't seem right waiting on a step son."

"Wish you wouldn't call me that," said Porter, with a smile. "I'd like to think of us as friends."

Jesse sneered. "I think I'll keep the step mom thing. It keeps a little distance between us."

Porter lit a cigarette and set it in the ashtray. "One of these days you're gonna want a young buck like me. Just you wait and see."

"You know there are days I can't believe you belong to your daddy," she said. "You must have had one wild mother."

The smile on Porter's face disappeared. "Just keep my mother out of it."

"Oh, is this one of those my mother was a saint thing?"

Porter took a drag on his cigarette. "It just ain't right to speak ill of the dead."

"Suppose you're right."

There was a pause, then his trademark devilish smile returned to his face. "So, you're gonna work at the bar. I can't believe it. What d'ya think Pop will say when he finds out?"

"I'm hoping he won't find out."

"Someone in town will surely tell him."

"That's the point. Your dad never goes to town."

Porter leaned his chair back on two legs. "Got everything figured out, do ya? How do you plan to keep me quiet?"

Jessie frowned. She then picked up dirty dishes from the table and carried them to the sink. "You have no shame, do you?"

"Not when it comes to you, my dear," he said.

She walked over to the table to get the last of the dishes when Porter grabbed her leg and held it tightly.

"What a waste of good female flesh," he said pulling her leg.

"Let go of me," she barked.

"There's no way my old man is taking care of you."

Jesse jerked her leg but couldn't break free. "Let go of my leg!"

Porter got to his feet and wrapped his arms around her. "Come on, baby, I'm not going to hurt you. I just wanna show you a good time."

Jesse struggled to get free. "I'm warning you, Porter."

"We both know that you ain't had it in years," said Porter, his voice raspy with lust.

He tried to kiss her, but she dodged to avoid him. He tried again, and his open mouth found her cheek. Finally, she thrust her knee into his groin. He groaned and bent over in pain.

"If you ever try that again, I'll tell your father," she shouted angrily.

Still clutching his groin, Porter shouted back. "You do, and I'll tell him about you and Cletus Munson."

Jesse paused. Her face sobered. "What about Cletus and me?"

Porter forced a smile and sat down. "Thought you could get away with it, didn't you?"

"I don't know what you're talking about."

"It's a small town honey. Nothing goes on around here without somebody knowin' about it. You didn't think you could get away with it, did you?"

"Get away with what?"

"More than once, you've been seen comin' out of his trailer. Fact is, they say your dress is all wrinkled and your always-perfect hair is messed up. You tell me what you're doing over there."

"That's a lie, and you know it."

"Hell, Cletus hasn't admitted it, but he hasn't denied it either."

"How could you possibly trust what Cletus would say? He's wanted me since we were kids."

Porter grabbed a chair that was between them and threw it across the room. "Maybe I should take what you've been giving out to every guy in town."

Jesse grabbed a butcher knife. She pointed it at him with an outstretched arm. "Don't even try it, or I'll gut you like a pig."

Porter paused, then smiled. He snubbed out his cigarette and got to his feet. "Another time," he said. "We'll pick this up again another time." He then turned and walked away.

Chapter Two

In the small town of Steam Corners, businesses came and went, but Coonie's, the only bar in town, endured the passage of time. In fact, it was the only business that had never changed since its beginning nearly a hundred years before. The only change to the building in all those years was the addition of a kitchen. They were then able to serve meals in an effort to compete with the diner just two doors down the street. Then, after a few years, the specials of the day disappeared from the menu. Shortly after that, pasta dishes and Mexican foods were dropped as well. Eventually, they discarded the menu entirely and served only hamburgers and French-fries.

To most the residents of Steam Corners, anyone who was seen entering or leaving Coonie's was considered a deviant, immoral and a sinner. Those who worked there were destined to an eternity in hell.

It was early afternoon, and the temperature was already over a hundred. Jessie parked her pickup and walked inside the bar. It was dark inside, so she stopped at the doorway to allow her eyes to adjust. Despite the fact there was only one slow-turning ceiling fan, strangely enough, it was comfortably cool.

Quiet small talk came to an abrupt stop when she entered the room, but soon resumed when the intruder was identified.

Sitting at a table in the back corner of the bar, a big man wearing a cowboy hat leaned back in his chair. His name was

Earl Steelman. It was said that the town should have been named Steelman in his honor. Not only did he own Coonie's but nearly all the other businesses on Main Street as well. It was rumored that he owned a very lucrative gambling business and a few prostitutes as well. He was feared by many, loved by none.

"Jessie, over here," he shouted across the bar.

Jessie squinted into the dark, and then began to slowly walk in his direction.

Earl gulped from a bottle of beer and slammed it on the table. "Have a seat," he said pointing at one of the empty chairs.

"Getting an early start, I see, huh, Earl?" she said taking a seat.

"It's after six somewhere in the world. Want one? It's on me."

"No thanks."

"The last time you and I did some drinking, you got wasted."

Jesse smiled. "I remember."

"Never seen anybody so drunk."

"Oh, I wasn't that bad."

"I'll never forget that day," said Earl with a smile. "That was the day I almost got you in bed."

"You've been trying to get in my pants since high school."

"That's what you think. It started long before that. I used to peek in your bedroom window when we were just kids."

"You weren't foolin' nobody, Earl Steelman," said Jesse with a playful smile. "I knew you were out there. That's why I would take off my clothes real slow right in front of the window."

"I always hated it when you'd get down to your panties, and then pull the blind."

"I dearly loved teasin' you."

"I know for a fact I got my first boner lookin' in that window."

Jesse lit up a cigarette, her face sobered. "I wanna thank you, Earl, for giving me this job. I really need the money."

"Hell, I've been trying to steal you away from the diner for years. Someone as pretty as you is good for business."

"Sweet talk with get you nowhere, Earl Steelman."

"Sweet talk nothing. I'm tellin' you the truth. The ole boys that come in here just put in eight hours and ain't too anxious to go home to the missus. Most of them need a hundred proof encouragement and a beautiful woman to bring it to them."

"Well, that I can do."

"Don't hurt to flirt a little. Most of the boys are going home to a fat and one ugly woman. A little flirting from someone like you kinda eases the pain."

"Does that mean I have to flirt with the owner?"

"You can bring that on anytime, darlin'," he said with a smile. "I'll be listening to and believin' every word you say."

"Not that I'm expecting it, but what if one of your patrons has a little too much and gets out of hand?"

"Don't you worry none about that," said Earl. "Every night you'll find a man by the name of Buford Hayes sittin' at the end of the bar. He sits there all alone with an empty bottle of beer right in front of him. He don't talk to nobody, and nobody talks to him. People are just plain scared to death of the man and good reason for it."

"I heard about this guy," said Jesse. "So he's really that tough."

"The few men who tried him are lucky to be alive today."

Jessie took a drag from her cigarette. "How is business anyway?"

"All things considered, pretty good," he said. "You know how tough it's been around here since the draught. Hell, they've even talked about closing down the mill. You know as well as I that would put half the town out of work. Yet, business for me is good."

"Guess people want to drown their sorrows."

"Lucky thing for me," he said.

"So when do I start?" she asked with a smile.

Earl picked up the empty bottle and handed it to Jessie. You start by getting me another beer."

It was early evening, and the bar was nearly full. There was quiet talk, clinking of glass, and occasional outbreaks of laughter. Jessie was serving a table when the front door opened. It was Porter. He staggered across the room and stopped behind Jessie.

"I've been drinking," he said with a slur.

"So I noticed," said Jessie.

"For that I need a good spanking," he said weaving back and forth.

"Go sit down at that table," she said pointing at the back of the room.

He turned and staggered towards the back of the bar. "Yes, Mommy," he said with a loud voice.

Jessie glanced at the other end of the room. Earl was motioning to her. She walked over to his table.

"Isn't that your boy?" he asked.

"He's my step son," she said.

"I'm sure it's no surprise to you that he's a bit on the wild side."

She glanced in Porter's direction. "You could say that."

"I suppose you know he's in here just about every night."

"Does he behave himself?"

"Gets a little rowdy from time to time, but what kid doesn't?"

"Don't hesitate to kick his ass out of here if he gets out of hand. Ain't got no business in here anyhow."

Earl stuck his unlit cigar back in his mouth. "As long as he behaves, I'll take his money."

"Thanks, Earl," she said. "I'll go talk to him."

Jessie walked over to Porter's table. The other waitress had already brought him a drink, and, despite his condition, it was half-gone.

He gulped his drink and looked up at Jessie, his head weaving from side to side.

"Well, if it isn't my absolutely gorgeous mother. Tell me, Ma, how do you feel about incest?"

"I'm not your mother and keep your voice down."

"Pretend that you are my mother. How do you feel about incest?"

"Will you hold it down, Porter? You're going to get me in trouble."

"You're avoiding the question, aren't you? I think it's because you're ashamed of your feelings."

"Will you shut up? You're going to get me fired."

"You shouldn't be ashamed of your feelings, you know. It's okay to have desires for your own son. It's best to keep that kind of thing in the family if you know what I mean."

Jessie sat down across from Porter. She leaned forward. "Now get this straight. I am your step mom, and that's only because I married your father. I could care less if you live or die, and if you try anything with me again like earlier today, you will die."

Porter took off his hat and dropped it on the table. "That ain't no way for kin folk to talk to each other. Actually, I think it's all a big front. You're playin' hard to get, aren't cha? That's it. You're playing hard to get. Makes it all the sweeter when it happens. Damn, girl, why didn't I think of this before? When it happens, it will be the best ever. Just think about it. Having sex with your mother, and her playin' hard to get.

Jessie leaned even closer and stuck a finger in his face. "Get this through your head, it ain't never gonna happen."

Porter leaned forward until his face was nearly touching hers. His smile disappeared from his face. It was if he had instantly sobered. "Now you get this through your head. It will happen. I guarantee it. You might as well relax and enjoy it, 'cause it will be the best sex you ever had. Oh, you might resist me to ease your conscience, but when we're done, you're gonna have a smile on your face that will have to be surgically removed."

"You know, I've always suspected it, and now I'm sure of it. You're a sick man."

"Go ahead and admit it. My old man has never taken care of you the way a man should. Deep down inside whether you want to admit it or not, you're crying out for a real man, a man who will bed you down and make your eyes roll back in your head."

"Oh, good Lord, Porter," said Jessie. "You wouldn't know the first thing about pleasin' a woman. You've never thought about anybody but yourself in all your miserable, worthless life. I have no doubts that when you're having sex the last thing on your mind is whether or not she's happy. It's all about Porter and Porter's needs."

Porter leaned back in his chair and smiled. "We shall see, darlin'. We shall see."

Jessie got to her feet and pointed at his drink. "Go easy on that stuff. You've had your limit."

It was nearly midnight when a stranger walked through the front door. The crowd had all but dispersed. Those left behind were either engaged in quiet small talk or nodding off to sleep. Porter was asleep with his head on the table buried in his folded arms. Jessie peered through the darkness at the man who was slowly walking towards her.

"Harrison…Harrison Benson. Is that you?"

He was a handsome man over six feet tall and neatly styled hair. "Jessie?"

He took her outstretched hand still uncertain of her identity.

"I thought you were in law school," she said with a smile.

"I was, and for some reason they gave me a degree."

"So you're an honest to God lawyer?"

"You could hardly call me that since I've never really defended anyone."

She pointed at a table. "Have a seat. What will you have?"

"Scotch on the rocks."

"Be right back."

Harrison took a seat at the table. He was loosening his tie when Jessie set a drink in front of him.

"What are you doing back in this town?" she asked taking a seat across the table.

"Kinda figured this one-horse town could use a lawyer," he said sipping his drink. "Hope there are others who will agree."

"Good Lord, I haven't seen you since high school, and may I say the years have been mighty kind to you," said Jessie.

"So, what about you?" he asked. "Been working here for very long?"

"It's my first day."

"I thought you were working at the diner."

"I quit after I got married."

"You married Frank Harlan, didn't you?"

"It's been five years."

"And he lets you work in this place?"

"He's out of town for the summer," she said. "Found work in Jefferson County."

"Things been tough around here?"

"The draught has all but killed the town. Can't grow anything, no water to keep livestock. People take any job they can get."

"Sorry to hear that," said Harrison. "It must seem like a shame to see the once powerful Harlan empire whither away. What happened to all of that Harlan money that everyone talked about?"

Jessie turned and pointed at Porter who was asleep at his table. "Old man Porter left it all to him. That's young Porter Harlan. He gets it next year when he turns twenty-one."

Harrison peered across the room. "Let me guess, he's a chip off the old, old block."

Jessie sneered. "Drinks like a fish and beds every woman in town."

"As I recall, old man Harlan was a fairly handsome man."

"Say what you want about him, but he was at that," she said. "The boy got his looks too. In fact, he's a spittin' image of his grandpa, personality, everything."

"Don't know whether to feel sorry for him or not."

"So, what about you? I heard you got married," she said in an effort to change the subject.

"My wife and child were killed in a car accident," he said matter-of-factly as if he had said it a million times before.

"They called it an accident, but I call it murder."

"Why? What happened?"

"A drunk hit her car so hard it was crushed beyond recognition. My son was with her. They called it an accident, went through the motions and the monster who took my wife and child from me had his license taken from him and was put on probation."

"Good Lord," said Jessie. "Why didn't they put him in prison?"

"For some reason, drunkenness exonerates you from guilt. In such a state, you're not responsible for your actions, so, you get a get-out-of-jail card. The man who killed my family is out in public ready to do it again."

"I'm so sorry," said Jessie.

"I guess that's why I became a lawyer. I surely can't do anything about it, but maybe I can better understand the law."

There was a long pause.

"Sorry," he said forcing a smile. "Didn't mean to dump my problems on you."

Jessie reached out and took his hand. "That's okay. I'm glad you told me. Makes me think you like me enough to trust me."

Harrison lightly squeezed her hand. "Oh, I like you enough. That's for sure. Always have. You were the prettiest girl in our class hands down. Had more than one dream about you."

"Why Harrison Benson. I didn't think you even knew I existed."

"Why would you say that?"

"You were the most popular boy in school. You played in all of the sports, president of our senior class. I was just a poor white trash girl from the other side of the tracks."

"Good Lord, there wasn't a boy in that school who didn't want you… including me."

"You're making me blush."

"You were and still are the most beautiful woman I ever met."

"Why didn't you ever ask me out?" she asked, slipping her hand deeper into his.

"I don't know. Guess I was scared you'd turn me down."

"Well, that's just plain silly."

"Well?" he asked.

"Well what?"

"Would you have gone out with me?"

She paused as if to build the suspense. "How long have you wondered about the answer to that question?"

"Just about everyday since we graduated."

"You really did have a thing for me, didn't you?"

"Yes, I did, now tell me if you would have gone out with me."

Jessie paused. "I should leave you to wonder."

"Aw, come on, Jessie."

"In a heartbeat. I would have loved to have gone out with you." Her smile disappeared and her face grew sullen. "In fact, I would still…"

Harrison pulled back his hand and got to his feet. "I'd better get going," he said. "It's getting late."

"You didn't finish your drink."

"Got a long day tomorrow, and if I don't stay home and unpack boxes, Tilly will do it all herself."

"Who's Tilly?"

"She's my cleaning lady, maid, cook, whatever. She and her eighteen-year-old daughter go wherever I go. By the way, they're black. How do you think the residents of Steam Corners are going to handle that?"

"If they are hired hands and not residents, they're okay," she said. "They'll be alright."

He smiled and lightly touched her shoulder. "Nice seeing you again."

"The pleasure was all mine," she said getting to her feet. "See you again?"

"You can count on it," he said and walked away.

Chapter Three

It was early afternoon and already the temperature was record setting. Jessie carried a tall iced tea to the front porch and sat down on the swing. She sipped her drink as she slowly pushed herself back and forth.

It felt good to be working again. She wasn't quite sure why. Seemed like just about anybody would have traded places with her. Everyday was all about shopping, eating or just plain relaxing. Didn't make sense to find happiness in waiting tables again. Must have something to do with being around people again. Got so lonely out there all alone on the ranch.

Jessie sipped her drink and set it on a small table beside the swing. Then something strange seemed to be happening. The sun seemed to disappear. She looked up at the western sky. Low-lying dark clouds were racing in her direction. She heard a low rumble in the distance and saw a flash of light. A wind gust sent dust and dead leaves whirling across the ground like miniature twisters. She could feel the cool air blowing in. Another gust blew her cotton dress to her waist. The cool air felt good on her legs. She glanced around. She was alone. She scooted out of her panties and dropped them on the floor. Jessie spread her legs wide. The cool air soothed her hot sensitive skin.

The clouds were soon over her head. Lightening bolts lit up the darkened sky as low rumbling thunder served as a warning of the approaching storm. Jessie wanted to take off her dress and let the gusting wind cool her whole body. She started to unbutton the front of her dress, then stopped. It wouldn't be right. What if someone pulled up in the drive? There would be no time to cover herself. With the wind and thunder, she couldn't hear any approaching vehicles. She couldn't take her dress off completely, but she could certainly let in as much cool air as she could. She finished unbuttoning her dress down to her waist. Already she could feel the cool air on her bare breasts. She pulled open her dress and faced into the wind. The air seemed to wrap around her ample breasts gently caressing them. Goosebumps appeared. Her nipples hardened. She felt a stirring deep inside her. She felt naughty yet vulnerable. It was if the wind was making love to her. The wind gusts came more frequently now. It was if it was pounding her, thrusting at her, trying to get inside her. She leaned back in the swing, her arms dropped seemingly lifelessly at her sides. She relaxed. The fight was over. She would let this powerful force take control. She slid down on the swing until she was nearly lying down. The wind pounded harder. She ran her hands over her firm breasts. Her nipples were harder and bigger than she had ever known them to be. Her hand drifted slowly down her stomach and gently caressed her inner thighs. Her legs twitched. She could feel her head pounding. She was about to explode. Her fingers slowly moved up her leg. Her index finger eased past the moist folds and thrust deep inside her. Still holding her breast with her other hand, she moaned and arched her back.

It was over in seconds. She went limp in the swing panting uncontrollably. A feeling of well being swept over her. Her body shuddered in the cool breeze that now had abated. The tail of the dark clouds raced overhead bringing sunlight once again.

Jessie's eyes suddenly snapped open. She glanced down at herself. For all practical purposes, she was totally naked. In an instant, the lust she felt turned to shame. She scooted up in her seat pulling her dress down over her exposed legs. Before she could finish snapping the buttons on the front of her dress, the door opened. It was Porter. Fortunately, he was holding his head and had his eyes closed, most likely in an effort to nurture a hangover. She had two choices. Either finish with her buttons or pick up her panties. She bent over and scooped up her underwear.

She turned to Porter. "What do you want?" she asked.

He pointed at the cleavage from breasts that were barely covered. "I want that," he said. "What have you been doing out here?"

"I was enjoying the cool air."

"You were exposed, weren't you?"

"Kinda."

"No, you had it all hanging out, didn't you?"

"Okay, Porter," she said. "I had it all hanging out. What can I say? It felt good."

Porter winced and grabbed his head with both hands. He sat on the porch steps. "Call me the next time, will ya? I don't care how bad of a hangover I have."

"If you won't respect the fact that I'm your step mother, at least remember that I'm married."

"Being married hasn't stopped about half the women in this town."

"You've had sex with married women?"

"Oh, don't act so surprised," he said. "Have you got any aspirin? The bottle in the medicine cabinet is empty."

"Who were they?"

"Who were who?"

"Who were the married women?"

"Sorry, but I don't kiss and tell. Now where's that aspirin?"

"Come on, Porter. All the crap I take from you and you can't do me this one favor?"

"You don't have any panties on, do you?"

"How did you know that?"

"You're sitting on what looks like a pair of white panties."

Jessie stuffed them out of sight. "So what? When I was a young girl, I never wore underwear at all."

Porter turned his body so that he was staring at her knees. "Spread your legs, and I'll give you a name."

She turned her legs away. "Grow up, Porter."

"You're begging for a name of a married woman I've had sex with, and you tell me to grow up?"

"That's different."

"How so?"

"Women need to know about these things."

"Tell the truth," he said wincing in pain. "It's juicy gossip."

"That's a possibility, now give me a name."

"Most of the names wouldn't surprise you, but I do have one name that would."

"Who is it?" she asked, squirming with excitement.

"Ruth Gordon."

"The mayor's wife?"

"The one and only."

"You screwed the mayor's wife?"

"She ain't all that bad either."

Jessie paused. "She's president of every women's group in town."

"Well, I can tell you one thing," said Porter. "I'm president of her fan club, 'cause I'd like to do her again."

Jessie kicked the floor to put the swing in motion. "You'd better stay away from that. Whatever you do, don't let the mayor catch you. He's nobody to mess with."

"So, what about you?" said Porter. "I hear you spent most of last night with an old boy friend."

"He ain't no boyfriend."

"Did you go to school with him?"

"Yeah."

"Did you ever date him?"

"Yeah."

"Then he's an old boyfriend."

"I dated a lot of guys, doesn't make them boyfriends."

"I'll bet he shows up again tonight."

"That doesn't mean anything."

"Listen, I'm the only one in town who goes there every night. He's going to show up, and he will ask you out," said Porter. "Trust me."

Jessie stopped the swing. "He wouldn't do such a thing. He knows I'm married."

"He'll disguise it," said Porter. "It won't look like a date, but that's what it will be."

"I don't believe it."

"Why not. Every guy wants to get in your pants. Why not this lawyer guy?"

Jessie paused and turned to Porter with a frown. "For the first time ever, you and I were having a normal conversation, and then you have to go get ugly."

"What'd I say? Every guy in town wants to do ya, including me."

"God, you're such a pig."

Porter got to his feet and started for the door. "I gotta find some aspirin before my head explodes."

It was early evening. The sun was already setting giving a slight relief from the searing heat. Jessie sat on the edge of the porch her feet resting on the wooden step. She stuck her index finger in her iced tea and slowly stirred the cubes.

Bright, fiery colors streaked across the western sky as the sun sank below the horizon. Jessie stared blankly across the backyard at the farm that was decaying little by little each day. Dried flakes of white paint lay scattered on the ground around the sides of the barn. The once neatly trimmed lawn was now knee high in weeds and grass that had gone to seed.

Jessie sipped her tea. It was sweet and tasted good on her lips. She never could make it as good as her mother's. That never made sense to her. It really didn't require a special knack for making tea, and, yet, nobody in town could make a tea that equaled hers.

Jessie loved her mother. She was a kind woman with strong virtues and a sense of discipline and fair play. Seemed like she could never measure up to her mother's standards. Seemed like somewhere along the way, she stopped trying. Too bad, she thought. Maybe if she had, things would be different today.

Life seemed much simpler back then. The sweet days of youth were fleeting and soon gave way to adulthood. She missed her mother. She missed her sweet tea. Why couldn't things be as they once were? Why couldn't her life be as simple as it was back then? If only she could see her mother and talk to her once again. Things would be better...so much better.

The screen door screeched, and Porter stepped onto the porch. Jessie quickly wiped her eyes.

"What's wrong with you?" he asked.

Jessie blew her nose onto a tissue. "Nothing," she replied.

He sat down beside her. "You've been crying, haven't you?"

"I got something in my eye."

"Come on," he said softly. "Talk to me. Something is wrong."

Jessie took a deep breath. "Just missing my mother."

Porter's smile disappeared. "I don't think I ever heard what happened to her."

Jessie ran her fingers through her long blond hair and leaned back. "It was a long time ago, besides, you don't want to hear about that."

"Yes, I do," he said with a solemn look. "I really would like to know more about you and your family."

She turned and stared across an open field. A gentle breeze stirred her hair. She missed her mother. In spite of the years that had passed since her death, she missed and thought about her everyday. Somehow it didn't seem right. To talk about her with others seemed almost disrespectful, and, yet, in her heart she meant only praise.

"She'd been working two jobs trying to make ends meet. Women didn't make much money back then, for that matter neither did men. A dollar and hour was not unheard of. She had just put in an eight-hour shift and was headed for her second job when she fell asleep at the wheel. She had done it before and got away with it, but this time was different. The guy driving that semi had the green light and never slowed down. He never saw her until her car was right in front of him."

Porter looked away. "Sorry," he muttered.

Jessie paused for a moment then shifted her weight on the hardwood porch. "What a loss. She was an incredibly simple woman with an incredible sense of dignity and morality. She was a far better woman than I've become."

"Don't say that," muttered Porter.

"I say it because it's true."

"I don't think of you as a bad person."

"You didn't know my mother...and you really don't know me."

"If you don't mind my asking, why was your mother working two jobs? Where was your father?"

"My father was bedridden with an injury. It wasn't work related and we had no insurance, so it was just a matter of time before we were broke. Needless to say, mother had to go to work. With me to raise and dad to nurse, she took on two jobs. During the day, she washed dishes at the diner, and at night she cleaned floors at the school.

There was a man who lived behind us in a one-room shack. He was an old man, someone said he was in his nineties. I think his name was Higgins. I don't think anyone ever knew his first name. Most everyone called him Mr. Higgins or just plain Higgins. Of course, the kids in town called him Old Man

Higgins. As I remember, he was one of those kind of guys whom always looked old even when he wasn't.

Anyways, Higgins didn't have much, just the few dollars he got each month from social security. It took care of the electric bill and bought him milk and cereal. That's about all he had to eat. He was happy though. Can't imagine why. There was nothing for him to do. He had a radio but didn't want to waste the electricity on it. His electric bill couldn't have been more than a few dollars. All he had was a refrigerator just big enough for a quart of milk and a few eggs, and a 25-watt light bulb. That was it.

In spite of all of our own problems, my mother felt sorry for old man Higgins. We barely had enough to eat, and, yet, once a week she would make a delivery to his house of a bag of canned goods, a loaf of bread, and once in a while when she could afford it, a small piece of meat."

"What did your dad say about all this?" asked Porter.

"Mother never told him. She knew he wouldn't approve, so it was our little secret. Actually, she never told me, but I had seen her more than once delivering the food."

"I'm surprised you didn't resent what your mother was doing. After all, she was taking away food that was meant for you."

"I suppose you're right," said Jessie. "But I loved my mother, and I guess I trusted her to do the right thing."

"Whatever happened to old man Higgins?"

"He died a couple years later. He left a note on the table that left all his belongings to mother. Wasn't much, but it was all he had."

"Didn't your father wonder why he left everything to your mother?"

"Dad died a few months before Higgins," said Jessie. "His death was ruled an accidental overdose, but I know different. A doctor had told him he would never walk again. I know my father. He was a proud man. He would never want to be a burden to mother."

Jessie wiped her eyes, took a deep breath and turned to Porter. "All these years I've known you, I have never seen you like this."

"What can I say? I'm a sensitive guy," he said with a smile.

Jessie laughed aloud. "Thanks, Porter for listening to me. Every girl needs a cry every once in a while."

"I understand that," said Porter. "I haven't stopped crying since the Yankees lost the World Series."

Jessie got to her feet. "There's hope for you yet."

"Oh, let's don't go that far," said Porter. "I'm still the jerk you've always known."

It was after dark when Jessie walked through the front door of Coonie's. The crowd was small, the mood quiet. She glanced around the room. A few of the regulars were sitting at the bar; otherwise, the place was nearly empty.

"Hey, little darlin'," shouted Earl Steelman from his table at the back of the room. He held up an empty beer bottle. "Bring me a cold one, will ya, Hon?"

Jessie passed by the bar where a cold beer was already waiting. She set it on the table and took a seat.

"Business seems a bit slow," she said glancing around the room.

"It ain't Friday," he said with his booming voice. "Two days to go."

"Huh?"

"Friday is payday, and that means let's go spend it."

"That sounds depressing," said Jessie.

"What d'ya mean?"

"Seems so irresponsible to just blow your money like that, instead of saving it."

"I like to think of it as a redneck holiday, and the best part is there's one per week, and even better they spend that money here."

"Spoken like a true businessman."

Earl gulped his beer. "Ain't it the truth?" he said. "You look a little down-in-the-mouth. Why don't you go get something to drink on me?"

"No, thanks," she said lighting a cigarette. "I'm working tonight."

"How were the tips last night?"

"Twenty bucks, and Cletus owes me."

"Good luck on that," said Earl with a grin. "Cletus owes everybody."

"Hope to do better tonight," she said getting to her feet. "Guess I'd better get started."

"If you need anything, just holler," said Earl turning back to his paperwork.

Jessie paused. She was still standing next to Earl's table.

Earl looked up. "Something on your mind?"

Jessie forced a smile. "Earl, I don't know what your dress policy is, but I'm not wearing a bra. It was already after dark, and I was so hot."

Earl laughed and quickly glanced at her chest. "Honey, I encourage anyone who looks like you to shed as much clothes as you can. It's damn good for business. Oh, don't get me wrong. There will be plenty enough wives who will have their noses outta joint, but there are a whole hell of a lot more horny men who will appreciate the view."

"Thanks, Earl," she said and walked away.

The evening was slow for Jessie. A few more of the regulars stopped in for one drink and were on their way. At no time, were the stools at the bar completely filled, and none of the tables were occupied for more than a few minutes.

It was nearly midnight when he walked through the front door. Just as Porter had predicted, Harrison Benson had returned to the bar. He was less than average in height, slender build and was always well dressed. His fair skin and delicate features suggested a life of ease free of hard labor. He took a seat at a table near the front of the bar.

"We meet again," said Jessie wiping his table with a damp rag.

"Hi, Jessie," he said with a smile. "Nice to see you again."

"What can I get you?" she asked.

"A beer would be great."

"Be right back."

Jessie swung by another table and picked up dirty plates and glasses on her way to the bar. She filled a frosted mug with beer and returned to the table.

"Getting settled in?" she asked.

"Actually, that's one of the reasons I stopped in," said Harrison. "I'm not very good at arranging furniture and wondered if you would stop over sometime. Women always seem to know best about such things."

Jessie forced a smile. "Oh, I don't know…"

"Oh, I'm sorry. You being married and all probably wouldn't look good here in a small town."

"Yeah, you're right," she said with a devilish look on her face. "What time would you like me to come over?"

"Are you sure?"

"Yeah, I'm sure," she said. "Girl has to keep her reputation intact."

Harrison gulped his beer and got to his feet. "Late afternoon would be fine."

"Hey, where are you going?" she asked.

"It's late, and, besides, all I wanted was to see you."

"Then, I'll see you tomorrow."

Harrison turned and walked out the door.

It was near closing. The last of the patrons were walking out the door. Jessie was wiping down the bar when Earl leaned back in his chair.

"Hey, there, Lil' Darlin', bring me a bottle of the good stuff," he said. "And bring two glasses."

Jessie knew what the good stuff was. Earl loved Crown Royal and kept cases of it in the backroom. She carried the bottle and two glasses across the room and set it on his table.

"Sit down, girl," he said. "I don't want to drink alone."

"It's late, Earl," she said.

"What are you talking about? We still got a half hour before closing." He poured two drinks. "Here, this will get you where you need to go."

"I don't think I ever had any Crown Royal before." She sipped the drink. "Damn, that's good stuff."

"How come that old man of yours never got you any?"

"Frank doesn't drink."

"He doesn't? Hell, that don't sound American."

"He ain't never even tried it."

Earl gulped his drink. "Don't know what he's missin', does he?"

Jessie took another sip. "This stuff is so smooth."

"Drink up, girl," said Earl filling the glasses. "We got this whole bottle here to kill off."

"Must be terribly expensive."

"Are you enjoying it?"

"Yes."

"Then don't worry about it," he said. "It wouldn't hurt you none if you untied a few of them knots."

Jessie gulped her drink. "What are you talking about?"

"You just look like you might need to unwind," said Earl. "You seem tense or upset about something."

"You might be right."

Earl filled her glass again. "Must be hard on you with Frank gone."

She leaned back in her chair. "Yeah, I miss him a lot."

"Pretty young thing like you must miss havin' a man carry you off to bed."

"Oh, Frank isn't that kind of guy," she said, her words slurring already. "He loves me. I got no doubt about that, but in his own way."

"In other words, you ain't getting any."

Jessie filled her glass and took another drink. "Why? You applying for the job?"

Earl reached out and placed his hand on top of hers. "That I am, darlin'," he said with a sober voice.

Jessie set her drink on the table and leaned back. Her head was spinning from the alcohol. It had all been light-hearted banter until now. Even in her drunken stupor, she could see that he was serious.

"Think you're man enough?" she asked with a smile.

Earl tightly gripped her hand. His smile disappeared. "I know I'm man enough."

It was about that time that the other waitress started towards the front door. Earl bolted across the room to let her out. He said his good nights, let her out and latched the door behind her.

"We're all alone," he announced with a smile.

Jessie pointed at a chair next to hers. "Come and sit down next to me."

Earl slowly swaggered across the room. Beads of sweat erupted on his forehead. He had thought about this moment ever since he met her. Fantasies of her swirled in his mind. His head throbbed with excitement. He pulled up a chair and sat next to her.

"Now where were we?" he asked, his voice raspy.

"You were telling me how much of a man you are."

With one hand, Earl began rubbing her back and shoulders. Jessie moaned in approval.

"Tell me something," said Earl. "How married are you?"

"What do you mean?"

"You know what I mean."

She held up her hand. "I have a ring."

Earl sneered. "That don't mean anything."

He ran his hand over her shoulders and lightly caressed her bare arm.

"I didn't think that would make much of an impression," she said closing her eyes. "Damn, that feels good."

He ran one finger lightly over her cheek. "I know something else that would feel even better."

Jessie said nothing. She groaned as he lightly swirled his finger over her bare skin.

"Relax," he said. "You seem tense."

"It's been a long time."

"A long time for what?"

"Since…since a man has touched me."

"How does it feel?"

"Incredible," she said with a slur. "Simply incredible."

Earl glanced at her chest. Her firm, ample breasts strained the buttons on her blouse. He slightly lowered his head to peek through the openings at the soft skin. Earl swirled his finger down her arm to the soft skin on the inside of her elbow. She was panting now. Her eyes were closed and sweat trickled down her neck and disappeared behind her blouse. He could see the outline of her hard nipples. His finger was only inches away. So far, it had all been innocent play. He had not crossed any line, but that was about to change. His head throbbed. He could feel the blood pounding through his veins.

Earl reached over and lightly touched the side of her breast. It was firm and yet soft to the touch. Jessie jerked. She moaned and arched her back. Earl withdrew his finger. He wasn't sure.

Was that a cold reaction? Was she pulling away? Then, Jessie moved her chair closer and turned in his direction. "Please," she uttered softly.

Her breasts were right in front of him, heaving now from her heavy breathing. Earl could see her nipples through the sweat-soaked blouse. He could feel his manhood throbbing in his pants. He reached over and gently unbuttoned the top button of her blouse. He glanced at her face for a reaction.

"Faster," she muttered.

His hands trembled as he fumbled with the remaining buttons. When he finished with the last one, he slowly pulled her blouse open. Cool air from a slow-turning ceiling fan washed over her exposed breasts making her nipples even harder and leaving small bumps on her skin.

In spite of his gruff exterior, Earl knew women and he knew what pleased them. He reached over with both hands and lightly touched the sides of her bare breasts. She jumped slightly but moved even closer. He slowly moved his fingers to the underside of her breasts, caressing the soft skin, coming close to her nipples but never touching them. He then formed circles around the breasts even closer to her nipples, occasionally, brushing them as if by accident.

By then, Jessie's chest was rising and falling as she gasped for air. Earl firmly grasped her ribcage and leaned towards her. He lightly touched her lips with his. As she moved closer to kiss him, he pulled away, then lightly, hovered his lips over hers.

Crazed with lust, Jessie pulled him close to her, savagely kissing his lips. The taunting and teasing was over. Earl wrapped his arms around her and kissed her long and hard. Still locked in a tight embrace, Jessie slid her cotton blouse over her shoulders and let it fall to the floor. Earl fumbled with his belt sending his pants sliding down his legs. He stepped out of them just as she did hers.

"Take me now," she said with a raspy voice. "I don't care where, just do it."

Earl picked her up and sat her on the edge of the table. He grabbed her ankles and slid her closer to the edge. Jessie lay back on the table. She wanted to scream. Her whole body was on fire. He had to do, and he had to do it now. What was he waiting on? She could feel hot liquid as it dripped from the tender folds of her skin and onto the floor. He wasn't going to tease her again. He wouldn't do that. He couldn't.

Then it happened. She felt his strong, hard manhood as it slid, effortlessly, into her. She screamed with pleasure. Her whole body screamed with pleasure. It was obvious that the teasing and taunting of foreplay was over. He was at the right height and could easily slam it deep into her. She screamed with pleasure at every thrust that he made.

Her first orgasm came within seconds, the second and third minutes later. He picked up speed, slamming home even faster. Jessie was delirious with pleasure. Her orgasms seemed to be coming with every thrust. It went on for what seemed like an eternity. She had never experienced anything like this before. He was man enough. That was for sure.

Just as she was about to pass out, he slowed his movement. He leaned his head back and emitted a guttural, almost primal growl. She felt him pulsating inside her, then, slowed to a stop.

"Good Lord, that was incredible," he said still holding her legs.

Jessie ran her hands through her soaking wet hair. "I thought I was going to pass out."

He stepped back and helped her to a sitting position. "If there was anybody next door, I'm sure they thought from the way you were carrying on that someone was killing you."

She leaned on his shoulder. "Where did you learn all that?"

"What are you talking about?"

"Most men don't know the first thing about taking care of a woman," she said kissing his face and neck. "You had me on fire."

"One of my wives used to tell me what felt good and what didn't," he said wiping the sweat from his face. "Ain't no secret to it. You just gotta tell us what ya like."

"You make it sound so easy."

"It is once a fella understands the plumbing of a woman."

"Are you still married to Martha Rose?"

"Separated and soon to be divorced," he said.

"Sorry," said Jessie. "What happened?"

"Nothin' in particular," he said shifting his weight. "We just had different ideas about sex. I thought it was a good thing, and she didn't."

"Well, Earl, why did you marry her if she didn't like sex?"

"Good Lord, missy, she was a proverbial slut right up until the time she walked down the aisle. I should have guessed that smile on her face meant that she would never have to do that shit again."

Jessie laughed.

"Ain't funny. If it weren't for a little filly on the other side of town that takes care of me from time to time, I'd go nuts."

"Who is she?"

"Who is who?"

"The little filly on the other side of town. What's her name?"

"I ain't tellin' you."

"Why not?"

"She's got a little business going, and I don't want to mess that up. Besides, it's none of your business."

"It's Mavis Red, ain't it?"

"Hell, no. I wouldn't do Mavis Red for anything."

"Why not?"

"She's got a face that would stop a clock."

"I didn't think that made any difference."

"Does to me."

"She's got a great little body," said Jessie. "Why don't you just turn her around or put a bag over her head?"

"Aren't we getting off the track here a little bit? After all, Mavis ain't the one."

"Must be Peggy Sue Snider. Ya, that's it. I always knew she was a tramp."

Earl pulled on his pants and fastened his belt. "You need to get your sweet little ass on home."

Jessie pulled on her blouse and buttoned every other one. "You ain't denying that it's Peggy Sue."

Earl finished dressing and took her in his arms. "I'll see you tomorrow night," he said giving her a quick kiss.

Jessie smiled. "Looking forward to it."

Chapter Four

It was early afternoon, and with no clouds in the sky, the sun was once again scorching the countryside. With her morning chores finished, Jessie stepped outside on the front porch. There was no escaping the heat, and it seemed as if it would never end. The once lush green lawn was now parched ground with dust swirling in the wind.

Jessie sat on the porch swing and kicked it in motion. She smiled. The back-and-forth motion felt good. The subtle breeze it created felt even better. She kicked harder. The swing rocked from side-to-side as it made a wobbly arc. The rusted chains screeched hypnotically as the swing dipped and soared.

Jessie stared at the peeling paint on the porch railing. It wasn't always like this. There were days when this farm was the biggest and most productive in the county, and the house was the envy of every housewife in town.

They were better times, all those years ago. The grounds were kept neatly trimmed, the house and out buildings freshly painted every two years. It was a hard life with much to be done. The bunkhouse held twenty and was usually over its capacity. In spite of all the help, it seemed as if they could never catch up.

Jessie let the swing slow until it was stopped. She stared across the barren fields. It seemed so sad to watch it all crumble and fall. There will never be another harvest, nor will there be big gala parties at the house. The house will never be painted again, and the bunkhouse will remain empty. It was all coming undone, and Jessie was right there to watch it happen.

The front door swung open, and Porter stepped outside rubbing his eyes.

"Doesn't it ever bother you sleeping in 'til afternoon everyday?" said Jessie with a disgusted look.

"Should it?" he asked scratching his head.

"Normal people get up in the morning and sleep at night."

Porter sat on the edge of the porch. "Whoever said I was normal?"

"Good point," she muttered.

"So what are you doing out here all alone?"

Jessie paused then looked away. "Do you ever miss the old days?"

"What old days?"

"The days when this farm was alive, when there were trucks and farm vehicles coming and going, when the grass was green and the fence posts were white. Smells of dinner on the stove floated out open windows and across the barnyard, and as the sun went down laughter could be heard from the bunkhouse as the men settled down for the night. Do you remember those days? It wasn't that long ago."

"Yeah, I remember, but the draught killed this farm same as it did to a hundred other farms," said Porter.

"It wasn't the draught that killed this farm," she said. "It was dead long before the draught hit. Somewhere along the line your father lost interest. Your dad let it die."

Porter sneered. "Dad never was the farmer that Grandpa was. In fact, he was never the man that Grandpa was."

Jessie stiffened. "How can you say that?"

"'Cause it's true."

"Your father is a good man."

"He's got you fooled too, I see."

"What are you talking about?"

"He's lazy for one thing and a loser at that."

"How dare you to say that about your father. Right now, he's trying to earn enough money to keep the farm. That's more than you can say."

Porter slowly shook his head. "The only smart thing he ever did was marry you, and he's wasting that away."

"He's not wasting our…"

"Look at you," said Porter getting to his feet. "You're working in a two-bit bar, living in this run-down house. I'll bet you haven't bought a new dress in years."

"Times are tough right now," she said. "If we could only get some rain, things would get better."

"Whether it rains or not, nothing's going to change. This farm is dead, and you know it."

"I think you under estimate your father."

"And I think you live in a dream world."

There was a long pause, then Porter sat back down.

"By the way, what were you doing at the bar last night?" asked Porter with a smile.

"What are you talking about? I work there."

"It was after hours, and Earl's truck was there."

"So, it's his bar, and I was cleaning up."

"You were doin' him, weren't you?"

"That's a disgusting thing to say."

"The door was locked."

"Of course the door was locked. We were closed."

"It was 1:30. The bar closes at 2:00," said Porter. "And if there is anybody who would know when the bar closes, it's me."

"Earl was working on the books, and I was cleaning up," said Jessie looking away. "Don't make anymore out of it than that."

Porter snickered. "Hey, it can't hurt doin' the boss. It's called job security."

"God, you're disgusting."

"Hey, I'm the one who should be offended," said Porter. "You'll screw Earl Steelman but not me. Damn!"

"You are such a pig," she said and stormed off.

It was late afternoon when Jessie stopped in front of a small, white house on the other side of town. The shutters were faded and in need of repair. The gutters sagged, and the grass was knee-high. She checked the address. Sure enough, this was the place.

She got out of the car and started for the porch. She was wearing a low-cut, silky sundress with high-heels and a white straw hat. Her shoes clicked as she strutted up the walk. As she stepped onto the porch, the front door opened.

"Hi, Jessie," said Harrison swinging open the door. "I was expecting you."

"I guess so," she said. "I didn't even have to knock."

Harrison backed away to let her in. "Pardon the mess. I'm still unpacking."

Jessie followed a path among the boxes and found a spot on a sofa to sit. "Where's your maid?"

"She won't be here until next week and whatever you do don't call her a maid."

"Why not?"

"She likes to be called my assistant," said Harrison. "Don't know why, but I'm not man enough to correct her."

Jessie laughed. "Why is that?"

"She weighs about three hundred pounds and is as mean as a junkyard dog," said Harrison. "Whatever she wants, she gets."

"Is she married?"

"No, but she has a seventeen-year-old daughter by the name of Skeeter. I don't know if that's her real name or not, but what a beautiful girl. Her father was white, so her skin turned out to be this cream or mocha color. She's stunningly beautiful and yet a bit shy."

"Are they going to live here?"

Harrison cleared the sofa of boxes and sat down next to Jessie. "Just until she can find a place to live. She says that if she lived here, she wouldn't know the difference between her own time and when she was on the clock. Can't say as I blame her. Truth is I'd probably be having her do things on her own time."

Jessie glanced around the room. "You said something about needing my help."

Harrison glanced around as well. "I got to be truthful with you, Jessie," he said. "I made that all up. It was just an excuse to get you over here."

"Why did you do that?"

Harrison's face flushed. He forced a grin. "Ever since I saw you the other night, I couldn't stop thinking about you. I just had to see you."

Jessie smiled. "That's so sweet of you."

Harrison sat upright and moved closer. "I've had a thing for ever since high school. Did you know I used to walk by your house at nights? I don't know what I would have said if you had caught me."

"Were you peeking in my window?"

"No, I would never had done that. Thought about it. Fantasized about it, but never really did it."

"You should have," she said with a seductive smile.

"Why?"

"I knew you were out there, and I would undress in front of my bedroom window with the lights on."

"Oh, dear God!"

"Did you know where my bedroom was?"

"Yeah."

"Why didn't you come around to that side of the house?"

"I couldn't have done that."

"Why not?"

"I would have been too scared of getting caught," said Harrison. "Don't forget, your father was the sheriff in town."

"Yeah, you're right. He probably would have shot you."

"That thought crossed my mind."

"You sure missed a great show."

"You know, it's funny," said Harrison. "I don't remember a time I didn't think about you."

There was a pause. Harrison stared into her eyes. They were blue eyes, the brightest blue eyes he had ever seen. A gentle breeze from the open window scattered her blond hair. She swept it back but left sweat-soaked strands covering her face.

His hands trembling, Harrison wiped sweat from his forehead. "God, you're beautiful."

"Thanks," she said, still staring at him with slightly parted lips.

Harrison could feel his own heart pounding beneath his chest. "Good Lord, you're driving me nuts."

"Why? What's wrong?"

He jumped to his feet. "You're so incredibly beautiful, so sexy. I can't stand it."

"So, why don't you do something about it?"

Harrison froze. He was standing over her and could see the curves of her breasts as they disappeared into her sundress.

"You're not wearing a bra, are you?"

"Too hot. I don't wear underwear when it gets this hot."

"You're not wearing any underwear?"

She swept the few strands of hair from her face and smiled as she looked up at him. "Like I said, it's too hot."

Harrison ran both hands through his hair and took a deep breath. "Wanna see the rest of the house?"

"Sure," she said and got to her feet.

He led her through a doorway and into the kitchen. They stopped and looked around. A door on one of the cupboards was hanging by one hinge. The linoleum floor was ripped obviously from moving a large appliance, and the sink was full of dirty dishes.

"Got a lot of work to do," he said.

"Could use a woman's touch," said Jessie.

He then led her through an empty dining room, down a hall to the bedrooms.

"I have three bedrooms," he announced.

"Which one is yours?"

"This one," he said pointing at the one at the end of the hall.

"I was hoping we would end up here," she said. She walked down the hallway, opened the door and stepped inside. Boxes were stacked at one end of the room, and at the other end was an unmade bed. She walked over to a window and peered outside.

"The world doesn't look so dirty from up here," she said.

She sat on the edge of the bed and bounced up and down. She turned to Harrison. "You know I've done everything but throw myself at you. Not interested?"

Harrison paced the floor. "No. Well, actually, yes," he said, his voice cracking. "I mean I've always wanted you, but I can't."

"This isn't doing my ego any good," she said. "Is it something I've said? Not pretty enough for you?"

"It's nothing like that."

"Then what is it?"

"You're married."

"So?"

"Doesn't that make it adultery?"

Jessie smiled. "How does that work? We know it's adultery for me, but you aren't married. Does that make it adultery for you or just getting a stranger?"

Harrison paced in a small circle and stopped in front of her. "Wanna drink?" he asked.

"Sure," she said and followed him into the kitchen. She sat at the table while he dropped ice into two small glasses and poured vodka over them. "You're the first man to turn me down," she said. "I don't think I like that."

"Nothing personal," he said taking a seat across from her.

"I take it personal," she said. "I must be losing my touch."

"Honey, I've wanted you for most of my life. Believe me, that haven't changed."

With one finger, Jessie stirred the ice in her glass. "Then what is it?"

"I know I shouldn't let it bother me. Happened so long ago."

Jessie bristled with excitement. "Come on. Tell me."

"It's nothing much. I should get over it and get on with my life."

"Don't stop now."

Harrison turned away. "My father died when I was young. Actually, I can't remember his face. I made a point to remember, but it was so long ago. I still carry a picture of him in my wallet, so I won't forget, but even it has faded so much. It was years later when my mother started dating again. Men came in and out of our lives. Some I liked, some I didn't. Then one day, she found the man of her dreams and announced their impending marriage. I was happy for ma. After all, I didn't want her to live alone after I moved out. Nobody wants that, but there was something about that guy I didn't like. Could have been his drinking, since Pop never touched the stuff. I wasn't quite sure what to make of the guy. Even though I was just a kid, I pretty much guessed that his drinking seemed a bit abnormal. I hardly ever saw him sober, and to tell you the truth, he was about as loud and obnoxious as could be.

Be that as it may, Ma married him just the same. I don't know whether she figured she could change him or simply that it wasn't a problem. Either way, she would later discover what a mistake she had made. At first, he was a pretty good guy. Didn't even drink that much, but after a few years, his real identity showed up.

He didn't beat mother all that much in the beginning. I guess because he wasn't drinking. But that all changed. Seemed like within a year or two, he was drunk all the time. And then the beatings started. I tried to stop him once, and he nearly killed me. God, I hated that man."

Harrison paused as he shook a cigarette from a pack and stuck it in his mouth. He stuck a match to it and inhaled deeply.

"I'm sorry about your mother, but what does this have to do with anything?" asked Jessie.

Harrison inhaled again and set the lit cigarette on the edge of the table.

"It was a cold day in the fall. I remember thinking that I wished it would snow. I always figured that if you have to endure the cold, it might as well snow. The son-of-a-bitch came home late that day. I remember that because it was after dark. We had eaten, but mother had left something for him warming on the stove. Unfortunately, by the time he got home, it dried up and had even burnt in a few spots. He was drunk as usual and was enraged when he found out about dinner. He hit her once, and she flew across the kitchen. That was bad enough but not as bad as what he did next. She was still on the floor when he asked her if she knew where he had been. She didn't have to answer him. He told her that he had been over at Mavis Red's house having sex with her. He must have hated her a lot to tell her that. My mother just stared at him. She was still sitting on the floor. I think she was in shock, not over the fact that he had committed adultery, rather that he hated her so much that he rubbed it in her face that day."

"Whatever happened to him?"

Harrison picked up his cigarette and took a drag from it. "He went to prison for killing my mother."

"Oh, dear God!" said Jessie. She dragged her chair around the table and sat next to Harrison. "What happened?"

"My mother forgave him for his affair with Mavis Red. Why, I will never know. She couldn't have still been in love with the man. It's a mystery to me why people do what they do especially when it comes to affairs of the heart. Anyway, months passed since the Mavis Red incident. I thought things were getting back to normal. In fact, he seemed to be sober more often than he was drunk. It was nearly midnight before he came home that night. I was on a date and hadn't come home yet, a fact that has caused me great remorse and many regrets over the years. My curfew was midnight, and if I had come home when I was told to, my mother might be alive today."

"Did he really kill her?"

"I came home around one and found my mother on the floor with a butcher knife in her back. He never did explain what happened even during his trial. It wasn't like he tried to cover-up what he had done. His fingerprints were all over the murder weapon.

"Now you've been properly introduced to the skeletons in my closet. As you can see, from my limited experience with adultery, it has an ugly face. There was, however, some good that came out of all this. Sitting through the trial, I was inspired to become a lawyer. Whether or not that was a blessing remains to be seen.

He gulped down his drink and reached for the bottle. "Have another?" he asked.

Jessie finished hers and set her glass on the table near Harrison. "Sure."

He poured vodka over the half-melted ice cubes in her glass. "I bared my soul," he said. "How 'bout you?"

Jessie sipped her drink. "Not much of a story. Trashy girl from the wrong side of the tracks marries rich guy, then rich guy turns poor."

"Trashy?" said Harrison. "I never considered you trashy."

"Yes, you did," she said. "You were no different than the others."

"Did I ever call you that?"

"No, but I know you thought it."

"I always considered you to be one of the sexiest girls I had ever seen, but I never thought of you as trashy."

"You never asked me out," said Jessie. "You dated every other girl in our class, but never once did you ask me out."

"I guess I was afraid."

"Afraid of what?"

"Afraid you'd turn me down."

Jessie lifted her glass and finished her drink. "Must not have wanted me all that much."

Harrison refilled her glass. "You have no idea. I used to fantasize about you."

"Oh? And what kind of fantasy might that be?"

"The usual for a teenage boy," he said. "You taking your clothes off in front of me."

Jessie gulped her drink and turned to face Harrison. She smiled and bent forward revealing her breasts. "You mean you didn't have any fantasies about looking down my dress?"

Harrison glanced at the gaping top of her dress. Her breasts looked tanned and silky smooth. They were full and looked firm to the touch. Jessie jerked her body sending them lightly swaying beneath her.

"Good Lord," muttered Harrison from a trance-like state. He took a deep breath and wiped his forehead.

Jessie slid back her chair. "Maybe you dreamed about seeing my legs, and since I don't wear underwear..." She then pulled her dress up to her thighs.

Harrison glanced down at her legs. They were long and lean. She had pulled her dress up to her hips, but a fold of it drooped between her legs. His head was throbbing, his hands shaking. He wanted desperately to reach over and rip her dress from her body. Jessie took his hand and gently placed it on her leg just above the knee. Her skin was soft, and yet he could feel lean muscles.

"Ever dream about doing that?" she asked, her words slurring from the drinks.

Harrison said nothing. Beads of sweat formed on his forehead. Slowly, she pulled his hand further up her leg. He could feel wispy hairs touching the back of his fingers. He could feel blood pounding through his veins. He was so close. So close. Just a flinch, and he would be touching it. He had thought about, dreamed about this day for so many years. She was so beautiful, so sexy. He never dreamed he would ever have a chance.

"Go ahead and touch it," she said with a soft almost throaty voice. "You had to have dreamed about that."

Harrison gripped her leg in an effort to keep himself from doing it.

She leaned back and spread her legs.

"Good Lord," he muttered and tightened his grip on her leg.

"I don't think I ever saw a man with more self-control," she said. She then took his hand and gently placed it between her legs. He was panting now trying to catch his breath. He could feel the soft, warm skin at his fingertips. His index finger slipped between the folds of skin and buried deep inside her. She arched her back and moaned. Slowly, he pushed it in-and-out, Jessie moaning with every thrust. He pulled his drenched finger out and softly massaged the tender skin around the opening. Within moments, Jessie grew silent, and her legs rigid. She leaned back and spread her legs even further. Harrison picked up the pace rubbing his finger back and forth over the sensitive area stopping for only a moment to lubricate his finger by thrusting it inside her. He applied more pressure and could now feel her legs quivering. She was gasping for air.

Then it happened. Jessie had held back as long as she could and finally relaxed and let it happen. She screamed in total ecstasy. As her body relaxed, Harrison slowed his pace. He stopped as her body went limp.

"Oh, God!" she muttered, her eyes still closed. "Where did you learn to do that?"

"I can't really…"

"That was perfect," she said. "Most men don't have a clue."

"I'm happy that you…"

Jessie sat up straight and stared him in the eyes. "Now it's your turn," she said and got to her feet. She took two steps backward staggering from the drinks. She paused for a moment, then slipped one of the straps from her sundress over her shoulder. It fell to her waist nearly exposing one of her breasts. She slowly picked up the other strap and slid it over her other shoulder. It fell to her upper arm leaving her dress still clinging to her firm and taut breasts.

"Oh, God," muttered Harrison as he watched her hand slowly move to the top of the dress. He was nearly in pain as he watched this beautiful creature unmercifully tease him. With two fingers, she picked up the dress and eased it over her breasts. It fell to her waist exposing her upper body. She quickly slipped her arms out of the straps, and the dress fell to the floor. She was completely naked except for the high-heeled strap summer shoes she was wearing.

Harrison had had enough. He got to his feet and came at her with a look of determination. He took her into his arms and kissed her long and hard. His parted lips then moved to one side of her face, his lips lightly touching her cheek. They soon found her ear and lightly caressed the lobe. "I've got to have you," he whispered in her ear. She moaned in agreement. His lips ran down the side of her neck and moved to her chest. Slowly and with a gentle touch, he ran his parted lips over one of her breasts then lightly kissing the underside of it. Jessie was moaning loudly and squirming from one leg to the other.

Harrison scooped her up in his arms and started for the bedroom. He kicked open the door and gently laid her on the bed. She squirmed in anticipation as he pulled his tee shirt over his head and dropped his shorts to the floor. He slipped into bed and took her in his arms. It felt good to feel her naked body against his. A flood of teenage fantasies ran through his mind. It didn't seem possible that this could be happening. All those years wasted when he could have had the one thing he desired the most.

He kissed her with all the soul and passion of his being. His tongue darted in and out of her mouth with such a steady beat that it served as a prelude of what was to come. He gently ran his fingertips down her side, over her hips and down her leg. He then ran them very slowly up the inside of her slightly parted legs, pausing to lightly circle the small patch of hair between her legs. She couldn't stand much more. Her body ached for him. There had been men in the past who could excite her, but this man had her on fire.

He pulled his lips away from hers and once again slowly dragged them across her soft cheek, down her neck and onto her chest. Her nipples were hard and as big as she had ever seen them. She ached for him to touch them. It was if they were screaming for him to grab them and put them in his mouth. Instead he ran his parted lips around the girth of her breasts being careful not to touch her nipples. It seemed cruel to her, almost as if he were torturing her. Why didn't he grab her? She ached for his firm touch. Her loins throbbed in time with her racing heartbeat. She could feel his rock hard manhood against her leg. Why didn't he use it? Why didn't he take her like some kind of animal?

Harrison slid down in the bed. He then ran the tip of his tongue slowly down her side and across her flat stomach. Her legs sprung open as he rolled over between them. He put his face between her legs and lightly ran his tongue on either side of the patch of blond hair. She squirmed, uncontrollably, but held her position for him. With his two thumbs, he gently pulled back the folds of skin and ran his tongue over the tender skin inside. Jessie arched her back and gave out a loud moan.

Slowly at first, he ran his tongue over the top of the opening. She was nearly bouncing on the bed by then making it difficult for him to perform. He picked up the pace, flicking the area with the tip of his tongue. Moments later, her legs stiffened, her toes curled as her hips lifted straight up seemingly elevated out of the bed.

Her second orgasm came almost as fast as her first. This time she made no attempt to hold back. She screamed at the top of her voice. Her legs violently shook and shuddered. Her whole body seemed possessed. Harrison slightly backed away. He had seen women having orgasms before but nothing like this. Moments later, she fell silent. Her hips dropped back into the bed, and her legs relaxed.

She was exhausted and spent, but Harrison wasn't finished. He crawled up between her legs. He cupped one hand under her buttock and slightly lifted her off the bed. With an almost animal force, he slipped his hard member past her drenched lips and thrust it deep inside her. This time her moan was nearly a scream. He was a man obsessed. He had paid his dues. She was obviously satisfied. Now it was his turn.

It all ended in a fireball of pleasure and desire. His was a low, almost primal growl as she screamed with her third orgasm. They paused for a moment, then collapsed on the bed in complete exhaustion. Nothing was said. They lay there for several moments catching their breath and wiping sweat from their faces.

"I need a joke," she said at last.

"Huh?"

"I need to laugh."

Harrison leaned on one elbow. "What in the world…"

"You wouldn't understand. Just tell me a joke."

Harrison paused. "Do you know how to make a woman scream a second time after sex?"

"No. How?"

"Wipe your dick on the curtains."

Jessie started to laugh. Soon she was laughing hysterically and was choking for air.

"It wasn't that funny," said Harrison with a look of shock.

Within a few moments, Jessie began to relax. She wiped the tears from her eyes. "It's a girl thing. There are times in my life when I'm so happy I need to scream or laugh hysterically, and I guarantee three orgasms will get me there."

Harrison fell back on the bed. "That's the first time I've had…"

"You need not say anymore," she said, her face and voice sobering. "Hope we didn't bring up memories."

Harrison closed his eyes. He could see his wife sleeping in his arms after they had made love. "Sorry," he said. "Not a real good time to be bringing her up."

"You must have loved her very much."

"I once heard a song on the radio," he said as if he were thinking out loud. "I don't remember the name of the song, but it had lyrics that said something like, 'you're a part of me, I'm a part of you.' I actually cried when I heard it because it described us so well. The funny thing is I still love her. Hard to believe, isn't it? She's dead and gone, yet I'm still in love with her."

"I envy you," said Jessie. "A love like that is rare."

"I told you I didn't want to have sex with you because you're married. Actually, I think it's because I felt like I would be cheating on my wife."

"What happened? What changed your mind?"

"After all of the soul searching to find the right answers, it finally occurred to me that she would never want me to become some kind of hermit and not see other women."

"And when did you come to this conclusion?" she asked.

Harrison smiled. "About thirty seconds ago."

Jessie rolled out of bed and slipped her sundress over her head. "I gotta go. I'm late for work."

"Thanks, Jessie," said Harrison from across the room.

"You're thanking me for sex?" she asked with a smile.

"You know what I'm thanking you for," he said with a sober look.

"Glad I could help," she said and walked out of the room.

Chapter Five

It was nearly 7:30 PM when Jessie walked through the front door of Coonie's. She peered into the darkened room and could see that it was another small crowd. She felt a certain amount of relief since she was a half-hour late. She started across the floor when she heard a voice from the back of the room.

"You're late," bellowed Earl Steelman without looking up from his work.

She started for his table. "Sorry. I..."

Before she could take five steps, Earl hollered again, "Get your ass to work right now."

Something was wrong. Sure, she was late getting to work, but that shouldn't bother Earl. He was much too relaxed with his work policies. In fact, she wasn't quite sure if he had any policies. He was probably just in a bad mood. She decided to give him a little time before she talked to him. She stopped by a table, picked up an armload of dirty dishes and carried them to the kitchen.

It was later in the evening when Jessie decided to take a break. She snapped the cap from a bottle of beer and sat down at the bar. It had been over two hours, and Earl still had not said a word. Several times, he had summoned the bartender to bring him another beer, but other than that he had his head buried in paperwork.

Jessie turned to see him drain another bottle. She grabbed a cold one and started for his table. She had to know if his bad humor was directed at her or not.

"This one's covered in ice," she said setting the bottle on the table.

"Thanks," he said without looking up from his work.

"You mad at me?"

He paused, then made eye contact. "Disappointed, jealous, betrayed, and yeah, I'm a little mad at you."

"What did I do?" she asked taking a seat.

"I got word that you were at Harrison's place today for quite a while."

"Man, there ain't much you miss in this town."

"Well, is it true?"

"Yes, it's true. So, what?"

Earl slid his chair back and facing Jessie. "I know it's none of my business, but what were you doing over there?"

"Harrison asked me over to help him decorate the house."

"Is that all you did?"

Jessie's jaw tightened, her face reddened. "Like you said, it's none of your business."

"You screwed him, didn't you?"

"Once again, I have to ask the question, what's it to you?"

"I don't believe it," said Earl. "You make love to me one day, and fuck him the next."

"I still fail to see why that is any business of yours."

Earl's voice lost some of its anger. "I just thought that we had something more than sex. I thought we were starting a relationship."

"A relationship," she said leaning forward in her seat. "Earl, I'm married. I already have a relationship, such as it is. What we had was animal lust. That's all. What were you expecting?"

Earl fidgeted with a lit cigarette. "I don't know. I guess you might say I'm the fool here."

"You're not a fool, Earl. Why would you say that?"

"I guess…I guess I thought I had a chance with you."

"A chance for what?"

"I know I shouldn't say this, but I've been in love with you for a long time. I know I shouldn't be seeing as how you're married and all, but I can't help it. I've wanted you for a long time. I thought that maybe after what happened the other night, you might have feelings for me."

Jessie moved closer and took his hand. "Oh, Earl, I do have feelings for you. I think you're a great guy, but I love my husband. I know how that must sound, but it's the truth. What we did was wrong, but I don't regret it one bit. That was one of the most exciting things that ever happened to me."

Earl snubbed out his cigarette and leaned back. "Well, I guess I can't expect you to leave your husband just because I have the hots for you."

"I'm sorry, Earl," she said. "I didn't mean to lead you on."

"It's not your fault," he said with a smile of embarrassment. "I'm the one who jumped the gun."

Just then, the front door opened. Both Earl and Jessie looked up. It was Harrison. He took a seat at one of the tables.

"That son-of-a-bitch is not allowed in my bar," said Earl in a loud voice.

Earl started to get up. "I'm gonna kick his sorry ass…"

Jessie grabbed his arm. "No, Earl," she said. "You can't do this. People will talk. They will wonder what's going on, and I don't want anybody to find out about us."

"Or what you did with that asshole?"

"Let me handle this, Earl. I'll talk to him."

"Just make sure that he understands that he ain't welcome here, and if I ever see him again, I'll break his fucking neck."

Jessie walked across the bar and sat down next to Harrison. "Hi," she said very curtly.

"Hi, yourself," he said with a smile. He turned and stared across the room. "Is that Earl Steelman? I should go over and say something to him. I haven't seen him…"

Jessie grabbed him as he started to get to his feet. "No, you don't want to do that."

"Why?" he asked and sat back down.

"Well, I don't know how to tell you this, but he wants to break your neck."

"What?" said Harrison with a startled look. "What did I ever do to him?"

"It's not so much what you did to him, it's what you did to me."

"I'm not following you."

"Earl found out about you and me, and…"

"That happened just hours ago in the privacy of my own home."

"Earl has a way of knowing everything that happens in this town."

"Okay, so somehow he knows about our little meeting," said Harrison. "What does that have to do with him?"

"He's jealous."

"Why would he be jealous?"

"He has a thing for me."

"Well, what man in this town doesn't have a thing for you? That doesn't give him any special hold on you. Besides, aren't you pretty much already spoken for?"

"Please go, Harrison," she said taking his hand in hers . "I don't want any trouble."

Harrison grabbed her hand. "Well…"

"I'll make it up to you," she cooed.

He pointed a finger at her. "I'll hold you to that," he said and got to his feet. He turned to the table in the back corner of the room. Earl scowled at him. Harrison returned the stare for a moment then walked out the door.

It was nearly noon when Jessie rolled over in bed. The small fan beside her bed had somehow turned and was blowing away from her. Sweat pooled in her stomach and spilled over her side onto the bed. She reached over and turned the fan in her direction and settled back to cool off before getting out of bed. The cool breeze felt good, so she pulled back the top sheet exposing her naked, sweat drenched body.

It had been a long time since she had slept in that late. It felt good but made her feel guilty, even a bit evil as if she were doing something wrong. She couldn't think of any good reason for getting up. The laundry and dishes were done, and the house was reasonably clean. She could do some dusting, but what would be the point? Frank was away, and the only other person in the house was Porter and he certainly didn't count for anything. Besides, she owed herself a day off.

Moments later, she closed her eyes and was nearly asleep when she was awakened by a loud pounding on the door. Startled, she sat up in bed. Just as she did, the bedroom door burst open and Porter staggered in carrying a bottle of beer. Jessie quickly grabbed for the sheet to cover herself.

"Damn," he said falling back against the wall. "You're naked."

"What are you doing in here, Porter?"

"I always wondered what you looked like without any clothes, and I gotta say you're even better than I imagined."

"Get out of here, Porter!" she said her voice filled with anger.

Porter drained the bottle and tossed it on the floor. "You know, everybody else in town is getting a piece of you, and I think it's about my turn."

"What are you talking about?"

"Don't think I don't know what's going on, but that's okay as long as you share some of that stuff with me too."

"I'm warning you, Porter. You'll go to jail for rape."

Porter reached down and jerked on the sheet. Jessie held on tightly. He then grabbed a handful and ripped it from her hands. The force threw her back onto the bed. She scrambled to cover herself with her hands.

"Just don't seem right," he said fumbling to unbutton his shirt. "Givin' that shit out to every Tom, Dick and Harry, and I don't get any."

"You're my stepson, for Christ's sakes."

He managed to unfasten one button and started on another. "That don't make you blood kin to me."

Jessie became silent as she watched him struggle with another button. His eyes closed and his breathing slowed. She had seen enough drunks in her time to recognize what was happening. He turned and sat on the edge of the bed beside her. Soon his hands went dead and flopped down on the bed. His head bent over, and drool spilled from his mouth. Jessie eased him back until he was lying on the bed.

"Don't you go anywhere," he mumbled and passed out.

Jessie quietly got out of bed, slipped a sundress over her head and tiptoed out of the room. As she passed through the kitchen, she grabbed a half-cup of coffee left from yesterday and stepped out onto the porch. It was another scorcher of a day with only a slight breeze for relief. She sat down on the edge of the porch. In the distance were a few dark clouds that seemed to be marching at her with a purpose. At the time, it caused little concern. It was not uncommon to see a sky filled with dark clouds. Unfortunately, the hope of rain seemed to follow those clouds as they disappeared over the horizon.

Jessie was still aggravated with Porter. Seemed as if her whole life was filled with Porters, always wanting something. She should charge him with attempted rape. At least that might get him out of her life for a while. Even if he were found not guilty, they would have him locked up until the trial was over. Of course, no one in town would take her seriously. There'd be no doubt in anyone's mind that he did it, it's just that everyone liked Porter and would swear he was innocent. It really didn't make sense. He was arrogant, conceited and just plain rude to everyone, but it made no difference. They loved him anyhow.

Jessie sipped her cold coffee. Something strange was happening. The sky was a greenish yellow with ominous dark clouds. A strong, cool breeze kicked up making her hair stand out behind her. She smiled as she faced into the wind. It had been a long time since she had felt coolness on her skin. In spite of the threatening clouds and strange looking sky, she was mesmerized by the whole experience.

A newer pickup turned into her gravel driveway sending a whirlwind of dust at her. She squinted to see who had pulled up. The door swung open and Harrison stepped out. He gave a half-hearted wave and closed the door.

"Fancy seeing you here," said Jessie scooting over to make room.

The carefree, easy-going look on his face was gone. "How ya doin'as?" he asked as he stopped in front of her. He had the look as if he had something important to announce.

"Just enjoying the cool breeze," she said running her hands through her hair.

"Well, there's more to that breeze than just coolness," he said sitting down beside her. "The radio says that's one monster storm comin' and might even turn into a tornado."

She turned and smiled. "And you drove all the way out here to tell me?"

"Wasn't quite sure if you paid any attention to the radio or TV."

"You took the time to drive all the way out here to warn me."

"It ain't that far."

She turned back to the wind, her smile unchanged. "Can't remember the last time a man was so thoughtful."

Harrison stretched out his legs. "Oh, I can't believe that. Pretty girl like you."

"That's just it. Seems as if every man I meet will treat you just fine until he gets what he wants. Hell, bring ya flowers for that matter, but when he's done with you, all ya see is his backside."

Harrison turned to her and paused until he had her attention. "You ain't lookin' at my backside, now are you?"

"You're different, Harrison. Most men aren't like you. Trust me. I know."

"Maybe, you just haven't met the right man up 'til now."

Jessie paused for a moment, her smile got even bigger. "There has been one other man in my life."

"Oh, boy," said Harrison. "Do I want to hear this?"

"You know, when I was a young girl, I was probably the biggest fan of Roy Rogers in the world. I worshipped Roy Rogers. I read everything about him I could get my hands on, but I had never seen a Roy Rogers movie. It was killing me that I couldn't see a Roy Rogers movie. Here was my hero on the silver screen, and I had never seen him.

I remember I was about thirteen, and for some reason they were showing westerns all weekend long at the Palace in Marion. I wanted to go so bad, because one of those westerns they were showing was My Pal Trigger, one of the greatest Roy Roger movies of all time.

Pop had been out of work most of that year, and we were barely making ends meet. I was young and wanted to see that movie more than anything, but I just couldn't work up the nerve to ask him to take me. I knew that it wasn't fair for me to ask such a thing. All we were eating was potatoes and whatever we had canned from the garden.

It was a bitter cold Saturday in December. I don't think the temperature got above zero that day. We didn't have a movie theater in town, and the closest one was in Marion over twenty miles away. I remember how bad I felt since it was probably the last chance I would ever get to see a Roy Rogers movie in a theater. It would simply be another missed opportunity.

It was late in the afternoon when my father came up to me and told me to get my coat. He said that we were going to Marion to pick up my Christmas present. I was stunned but still took no time at all to grab my coat and follow that man out the door. I had no idea what he had planned, but it really didn't matter. Just a trip to Marion with my dad was exciting in itself.

Pop had an old pickup truck that was in bad need of repair. There were so many things wrong with it that we were surprised that it ran at all. But if the broken part didn't affect the drivability of the vehicle, fixing it was considered a needless expense. The heater hadn't worked for over a year, and for the most part, was not missed. But that day was different. It was bitterly cold, and the wind seemed to chill to the bone. In spite of my excitement, I was shivering just the same.

We didn't drive very fast in those days, so the trip to Marion took nearly an hour. I remember that I was nearly frozen when Dad stopped in front of the Palace Theater. I cleaned the frost from the window and looked up at the marquis. Sure enough. My Pal Trigger was playing.

I turned to Dad with a puzzled look. I couldn't understand why he would be stopping here. We were supposed to be picking up a present. He handed me a fistful of coins and told me that this was my Christmas present. There was just enough for me to get into the show and a little left over for popcorn. I remember asking him if he was going in with me. He told me that there was only enough money for me to go, and besides, it was my present. I asked him what he was going to do while I was gone, and he said he would be waiting for me in the truck.

I jumped out of the truck and walked into the theater with the coins still clenched tightly in my fist. I paid for my ticket and found a seat as close to the screen as I could get. It was a little early, so I had time to enjoy looking at the magnificent building. I sat there for probably fifteen minutes before the lights dimmed and the curtain pulled back to reveal the massive white screen looming before me. From somewhere in the back of the theater, there came the soft whirling sound of a movie projector, and suddenly images came to life on the screen.

The Coming Attractions were nearly finished when it finally hit me. I don't know whether it was because I was so excited about the movie or I was just plain stupid, but it hadn't occurred to me until that moment where my father was. My father was sitting in a pickup truck without a heater in zero temperature while I was sitting in a warm theater. How could I have been so selfish! How could I have let that wonderful man do something like that!

I never did enjoy the movie. I sat there watching the screen, but all the time I was thinking about my father out there in the cold. About halfway through the movie, I quietly slid out of my seat and made my way to the exit. As I approached the truck, I noticed that all the windows were frosted over. I opened the door and climbed into the truck. Dad was shivering so badly that he was shaking like a person with convulsions. He managed to ask me how the movie was, and I told him it was the greatest.

It began to snow as we made our way back home making the trip even longer. It was nearly two hours before we finally pulled into our driveway. I'll never forget that night. I only saw part of that movie on that frigid day all those years ago, but it was the best Christmas present I ever had, and I certainly will never forget it."

"That's an incredible story," said Harrison slowly shaking his head.

"Unfortunately, all of the men in my life fall short of my father."

"I can see why," said Harrison. "He set the bar kinda high."

Jessie turned and smiled. "Maybe not so high for you."

By then, the sky had turned dark. Dark gray clouds collided with each other as they rolled ominously across the sky. In the distance was a faint flash of lightening followed by a low rumbling of thunder.

Harrison glanced at his watch. "Gotta go," he said jumping to his feet. "Got my first client coming over."

Jessie slowly got to her feet. She wrapped her arms around him and kissed his lips. "Thanks for coming over," she said. "You restored my confidence in men."

Harrison glanced at the sky. "Are you sure you don't want me to stay?"

She lightly pushed him away. "Go on now. You don't want to miss your first client."

Jessie watched as his truck disappeared down the road. She sat back down on the porch. She couldn't stop thinking about him. He was a handsome man with a good job. Considerate of others. Hell, he had proved that today. Any other man would have wanted a reward for driving across town to warn her of bad weather. Not Harrison. He was above that. He truly cared. He seemed so different from what he was like in high school. He was quarterback on the football team which seemed to make him think he was better than everyone else was.

Just then, it started to rain. Thankfully, the overhang protected her. She could feel a cool mist on her feet and legs from occasional wind gusts. Within seconds, it was a downpour. Rain fell in torrential waves making it impossible to see even as far as the road in front of the house. Then, as quickly as it started, the rain stopped. It was if someone had turned off the spigot. The once blue sky had now turned colors casting a strange looking yellowish green hue over the countryside. Jessie sensed that something was wrong. She had never seen anything like this before. The barn, the road, the whole countryside had turned green.

Then, it happened. From the bowels of a dark, foreboding cloud, a small, funnel-shaped cloud descended. It snaked its way sideways across the sky then turned towards the ground. Jessie was stunned. She sat there in awe as this miracle of nature unfolded in front of her. She was aware of the potential danger but couldn't move. It was a once in a lifetime, and it seemed to fascinate her more than frighten her.

It was less than a mile away and moving very slowly. It seemed to pick up speed, and as it did it became darker in color almost coal black and extended out away from its mother cloud. As it neared the ground, dust and debris scattered violently from its path. It roared at a deafening pitch as it snaked across the ground ever widening its path.

Jessie finally sprung to life as it turned in her direction. There was no time to warn Porter, so she ran to the ditch by the road and literally fell face down in the weeded embankment. She grabbed hold of the edges of a partially buried rock. The roar of the serpent-looking monster sounded like a freight train. Jessie's body shook with fright as the tornado marched closer and closer. For the first time in her life, she feared that she was going to die. Nobody could survive the power and fury of this monster.

It was within a hundred yards of her when it suddenly changed direction. It turned ninety degrees and headed for the barn. Within moments, Jessie could sense it wasn't headed her way. She lifted her head just in time to see it plowing a path towards their hundred-year-old barn. She marveled at the power of this beast of nature. It was literally destroying everything in its path.

It was within a hundred yards of the building when the funnel suddenly lifted off the ground. It had exhausted some of its strength and was withdrawing back into the clouds. By the time it flew over the barn it was over a hundred feet off the ground. In spite of that, it still had enough power to rip the roof from the barn. It shot long strips of sheet metal sailing across the countryside as effortlessly as if they were leaves from a tree. Jessie ducked as she saw debris flying in her direction.

Seconds later, it was all over. The deadly funnel had retreated back into its womb, and the dark massive cloud sped away. Jessie slowly got to her feet and surveyed the area. Debris of all types and sizes was scattered about. The tornado left a twenty-foot swathe that meandered across a cornfield and onto their land. Fortunately, the only building hit was her barn, and then it only destroyed the roof. The walls were left intact.

Jessie heard a door slam from the house. She turned to see Porter carrying a beer and staggering across the yard.

"What the hell happened?" he asked gulping his beer.

"What d'ya think happened?" she said with a note of sarcasm in her voice. "A tornado slammed through here."

Porter stopped and stared at the barn. "Why didn't you come and get me?"

"Why? What would you have done?"

He finished his beer and threw the bottle on the ground. "I don't know...probably nothing."

She slowly shook her head. "Not a surprise."

He studied the barn and the pieces of metal roofing scattered on the ground. "Got a hole in the roof, I see."

"What do you mean a hole in the roof?" she said putting her hands on her hips. "The roof is completely gone."

Porter looked again. "Oh, yeah. You're right."

"Nothing gets by you."

Porter walked closer to the barn. "Guess I'm going to have to put a new roof on 'er."

Jessie shot him a sarcastic smile. "Put a new roof on it? You?"

"Yeah," he said stumbling and nearly falling down. "How hard could it be?"

"You have trouble feeding yourself," she said turning back to the barn. "I just hope it's covered by insurance."

Porter turned and started for the house. "I just hope we got more beer."

It was mid afternoon when Jessie showed up for work. The place was full of its regulars all clustered around the bar with no one sitting at any of the tables. Earl was leaning back at his table smoking a cigar.

"Can't make any tips this way," she said taking a seat at his table. "Everyone is at the bar."

"Marry me, and you won't have to schlep tables for tips," he said with a smile.

"Already married," she said lighting a cigarette.

"Not that anyone would notice."

"What's that supposed to mean?"

"Honey, a filly like you needs a stallion in the barn, and we all know Frank ain't no stallion."

"And I suppose you are."

"Hey, I know how to ring your chimes, and I got more money than God Himself."

In an effort to change the subject, Jessie turned to survey the room. "Know anybody who can put a roof on a barn?"

"Yeah, I heard something about a twister hitting your farm."

"Took the roof right off the barn."

"Are you okay?"

"Scared the hell out of me, but, other than that, I'm okay."

"Porter okay?"

Jessie sneered. "Would have been fine with me if that tornado had taken him right along with it."

Earl drained his bottle of beer. "Why? Ain't nothing wrong with that boy. A bit ornery maybe."

"I might agree with you if he wasn't all the time tryin' to get in my pants."

"Porter? You never told me that. How long has this been going on?"

"Nearly since I've known him," she said taking a drag from her cigarette. "He's a lot worse since Frank has been gone."

"You don't say," said Earl. "That boy always has had a problem keeping it in his pants."

"Don't I know it?"

"You want me and the boys to pay him a visit?" asked Earl. "We won't hurt him or nothing like that."

"Thanks for the offer, but I can still take care of the likes of him."

A devilish smile spread over Earl's face. He leaned over and whispered, "How 'bout y'all comin' over to my place sometime. I can't stop thinking about the other night."

Jessie laughed. "Earl, you do know how to woo a woman, don't you?"

"Why? What did I say wrong?"

"You don't get it, do you?"

Earl held out both hands. "Not really. I was just asking you to come over to my place. That's all."

"To do what?"

"I don't know. Have a couple drinks. Sit on the deck."

"And have sex," she said. "Isn't that right, Earl?"

"Hey, if that's what you want to do."

"Don't give me that," she said with a touch of anger in her voice. "That's why you're inviting me in the first place."

"So what if I am?"

"It makes me feel like a slut, Earl. A common slut."

Earl leaned back and crossed his arms. "You know, ever since you spent that evening with that lawyer fella, you ain't been the same."

"What's that supposed to mean?"

"I think you've got a thing for him."

"And I suppose you're going to remind me that I'm married and how immoral I am."

Earl smiled. "I would if I was that kind of guy."

Jessie smiled back. "You weren't worried about my morality the other night."

She leaned over to snub out her cigarette when the front door opened. She looked up to see a young black man step inside and ease the door behind him. He was tall, with broad shoulders and a slim waist. Jessie guessed him to have just entered his twenties. He quickly surveyed the room and took a seat at a table in the middle of the room.

The room went silent. It was if some alien had entered the room as all eyes turned to the newcomer. The only other black person who had ever been in Steam Corners was Harrison Benson's maid, Tilly, and she didn't really count. Since she was considered to be domestic help, nobody really considered her to be a resident.

Earl stared at the visitor. "Christ! What's he doing here?" he said as if he were thinking out loud.

"I don't know," said Jessie with a sultry voice. She started for his table. "But I'll find out." She strutted across the room with as much feminine charm as she could muster. "What'll you have?" she asked leaning back on one leg and placing a hand on her hip.

"Can I get a beer?" he asked.

Jessie leaned over the table. Her blouse billowed open revealing her breasts. "Gonna need to see some I.D., Honey."

The young man leaned over and pulled a wallet from his back pocket. He slid out a small card and handed it to her.

She tilted the card under the dim overhead light. "Edward Deacon," she announced.

"It's Spencer."

"What's that?"

"I like to be called Spencer. Edward seems a bit too formal, don't you think?"

She tilted the card again. "Says here you're from Detroit. Long way from home, aren't you?"

"Suppose you're right."

"Ain't gonna ask you what you're doing in a dump like Steam Corners, but it does make one wonder."

Spencer sat up straight in his chair. "I'm looking for a job and a place to stay."

"Seems like I heard there's plenty of jobs back there in Detroit what with all the cars they build."

"You're right. There are plenty of jobs if you don't mind living in Detroit.

Jessie handed his driver's license back to him. "The way I figure it, you've been old enough for a beer by six months. Be right back.

She walked over to the bar and requested a beer. Patrons swarmed around her whispering questions about the visitor that she couldn't answer. She dismissed them with a shrug, put the frosted mug of beer on her tray and returned to his table.

"I seem to be the talk of the town," he said as she set the beer in front of him.

Jessie laughed. "Wait until tomorrow. News travels fast in a small town."

"Has this town ever seen a black man before?"

"Once."

"What happened to him?"

"Disappeared."

"Did they ever find out where he went?"

"No one knows for sure. My best bet is the good ole boys had something to do with it."

Spencer frowned. "Let me guess who the good ole boys are."

"Sorry, but there are some people in this town who just can't let go of the past."

Spencer sipped his beer. "Why are you telling me all of this?"

Once again, Jessie leaned over his table, her breasts nearly falling out of her blouse. "'Cause you're a cute kid, and I wouldn't want anything to happen to you. Besides, that happened a long time ago. I would hope things have changed since then."

Spencer forced a smile. "And I hope you're right."

Jessie stood straight. "Enjoy your beer. If you need anything, just let me know."

Spencer gave her a courtesy smile as she walked away.

She walked over to Earl's table and took a seat.

"What's he doing here?" asked Earl.

Jessie sipped from Earl's beer bottle. "Says he's looking for a job and a place to stay."

Earl stared across the room at the young man. "A black kid looking for a job and a place to stay here in Steam Corners. Is he crazy?"

"I don't think so."

"Ain't nobody gonna hire that boy, and there sure ain't no place for him to stay," said Earl. "Where's he from?"

"Detroit."

"City boy to boot. Ain't no call for his likes to be comin' around a small town like this. He needs to get back up there with his own kind."

While Earl talked, Jessie stared across the room. "I don't know. This town could use a little shaking up."

"What d'ya mean? You approve of this boy comin' to our town?"

Jessie's eyes followed the outline of the young man's tee shirt as it stretched over the muscles in his back and arms. "I got no problem with it," she said with a sultry voice.

Earl turned to Jessie. Her eyes were narrowed; her smile seductive. "Christ, woman," he said out loud. "You've got the hots for him, don't you?"

"So, what if I do?"

"Well, I can give you two reasons; he's black, and you're married."

"Minor point on both counts."

"Have some self-respect, girl," said Earl, his voice getting louder. "Bad enough you'd fuck a fat old guy like me. You don't need to be getting yourself all wet over a black guy."

Jessie turned to Earl with a smile. "Why, Earl, if I didn't know any better, I'd say you were jealous."

Earl leaned over the table and grabbed Jessie's arm. "You listen to me, girl. There are people in this town who wouldn't approve of you right now."

Jessie pulled back her arm. "That makes us even, because there are people in this town who don't meet my approval."

Earl picked up his bottle of beer and pointed the neck at her. "I'm just telling you for your own good. You stay away from that boy. He'll get you in trouble."

"Earl, you know I don't like to be told what to do," she said. "Not by you or anybody else in this town."

Earl eased himself back into his chair. "Well, maybe he's just passing through.

Jessie knew better but decided not to tell him. After all, nobody in Steam Corners would hire a black man anyhow, so chances were real he would be moving on anyhow.

Spencer was on his third beer when he scooted his chair back from the table. He cleared his throat and announced loud enough for everyone to hear. "I'm looking for a job and a place to stay." The room went silent, and all eyes turned to the young man.

One of the older men sitting at the bar turned to his friend. "What did he say?"

Before he could answer, Spencer made the announcement again, this time even louder. "Does anybody have work for me and a place to stay?"

The place grew silent again. Some exchanged glances, and others stared at Spencer as if he had horns.

Spencer drained his bottle of beer and set it on the table. He started to get up when, suddenly, Jessie loudly announced, "I got a barn that needs a new roof, and I have an empty bunkhouse."

With wide-eyed faces, everyone turned to Jessie.

Earl grabbed her arm. "You don't know what you're getting yourself into," he said.

Jessie pulled away from Earl's grasp and walked over to the young man's table. She leaned over the table and smiled. "Got a place to stay for the night?" she asked.

"I was planning to sleep in my car," he replied.

"I live a mile west of town on 203. Look for the name, Harlan, on the mailbox. I'll be along after work."

Spencer scrambled to his feet. "Thanks, Mrs. Harlan. I really appreciate this."

"It's Jessie to you."

"Okay, Jessie," he said and turned to the door. "See ya later."

Jessie sauntered back to Earl's table, who, by now, had a disgruntled look on his face.

"I don't believe you sometimes," said Earl without looking up.

"Why? What did I do that was so terrible?"

"You hired a black boy for one thing."

"What's wrong with that?"

"If you hadn't, chances are he would have moved on. As it is, we can now expect to have a black resident in Steam Corners."

"Is that so bad?"

Earl smiled. "Ask the boys with the white sheets over their heads."

"Well, I don't care what they think," she said. "He needs a job, and I need a new roof."

Earl leaned back and stacked his hands behind his head. "Just where do you expect to get the money to pay for it?"

"Insurance is paying the bills."

"Are you with Bradley in town here?"

"Yes. Why?"

"He'll want you to hire a professional."

"He already told me to hire anybody I want."

"That didn't mean you could off and hire a black boy," said Earl. "He never would have agreed to it if he had known that."

"I don't think it's any of his business who I hire. Actually, I think this kid will do a good job. Besides, he's awful cute."

"I'm telling you for your own good. If you say something like that around the wrong people, they will come after you as well. I'm sure that some day it won't matter at all what color your skin is, but right now here in Steam Corners, it matters."

Jessie scooted her chair back to get up, when Earl grabbed her by the arm. "Any chance you want to stick around after work?" he asked with a smile. "Pay ya overtime."

"Sorry, but I have someone waiting for me."

"Oh, I see how it is," said Earl, his voice taking on a mocking tone. "Can't keep the boy waiting."

She pulled her arm away. "Really, Earl. I can't be rude to him."

"Let me get this straight," said Earl. "It would be rude to keep that boy waiting, but it's okay to turn me down."

"Earl, why are you acting like this? It was a one-night thing between us. That's all. I don't know why I even let you touch me in the first place."

Earl grabbed her again, this time with a vice-like grip. "Don't treat me like this, Jessie. I won't have it."

"You won't have it? Who do you think you are, Earl? You don't own me. You might want to remember one important fact, and that is I'm married.

Earl pulled back. "You might want to remember that when you go see that boy."

"And that's another thing, Earl," she said. "Stop calling him boy. They don't like being called that, and you know it."

"Well, he is a boy. Couldn't be over twenty-two."

"He's a man, Earl. In fact, I'd say he was more of a man than you."

"How can you say that? I could kick his ass in a heart beat."

"It's not about kicking ass. It's about having a little class and respect for people."

"Hey, I do all them things."

Jessie frowned and slowly shook her head. She got to her feet and stormed off.

The full moon that night brought a silvery glow across the countryside. As Jessie turned into her own driveway, she was relieved and a bit excited as she spotted a strange car parked next to the barn. There was no movement, just a lone figure behind the wheel. She parked her car and slowly got out. The door on his car squeaked with age as he got out of his.

"Have any problems finding the place?" asked Jessie.

"No, Ma'am," he said surveying the farm. "Big place you got here."

She pointed at the top of the barn. "There's where you're going to be working. Too dark to see, but the roof is nearly all gone."

"What happened?"

"Tornado came through here. Lucky for us, it missed the house; turned at the last moment."

Spencer looked at the house. "You said something about us. Is there a mister around?"

"My husband is away right now," she said with a nonchalant, uncaring attitude. "Won't be back for weeks. His son still lives here. He must be about your age."

Spencer covered a yawn with his hand.

"You must be exhausted," said Jessie.

"Haven't slept in two days."

"Let me show you where you'll be staying," she said and started for a smaller building near the back of the barn. She opened the door and snapped on a light. It was a long, rectangular room with cots on either side. At the front were a sink, a stove and a cupboard to store food. "Ain't much, but it's a place to lay your head. That small room at the back is a bathroom of sorts. Years ago, some of the boys got tired of the outhouse and built that bathroom."

Spencer stepped inside and scanned the room. "Looks great."

"You can eat with us up there at the house."

Spencer turned to her with a polite, gentle smile. "Mrs. Harlan, I can't thank you enough for this. I promise I'll do my very best."

"I'm sure you will, Spencer. You seem like a very nice young man."

"I hate to ask this and I promise it will never happen again, but would you mind terribly if I slept in tomorrow? It's only a couple hours until dawn, and I..."

"Don't say another word," said Jessie starting for the door. "You sleep as long as you want. Good night."

She opened the door then turned. Spencer had just begun to pull his shirt off. He stopped and threw her a sheepish smile. She smiled back then closed the door behind her.

Chapter Six

The next morning brought the promise of another hot day. By late morning, the air was heavy and the temperature was in the nineties. Jessie poured herself a cup of coffee and stepped out on the back porch. She sat on the swing and kicked the floor to put it in motion.

It had been a long time since there were men living in the bunkhouse. It felt good. It felt like the farm was coming back to life. She remembered when the farm was at its peak of production and nearly every cot in the bunkhouse was taken. The farm bristled with activity in those days of plenty. The work was unrelenting, and every man earned his pay. Seemed like there was never enough men to get it all done. Those were the days of lush green pastures and fields of corn that towered in the sky. Summer storms brought welcomed relief to the land and nourishment to the already bountiful crops. They were good times, times remembered by a few and forgotten by many.

A small, lazy whirlwind danced across the yard sending plumes of dust into the air. Jessie turned her attention to the bunkhouse. She wondered if her new hired hand was still sleeping, or quite possibly had awakened but was still lying in bed. He was probably stretching his legs to enjoy the coolness of the sheets. He was just relaxing. It was what people do from time to time. She knew he wasn't wearing a shirt, because, after all, he had started to remove that while she was leaving the night before. Without any doubt, he had removed his shoes and socks as well as his jeans before getting into bed. Most likely, he left his underwear on. All men do, or so she was told by Frank. There was a chance that he was naked. That was not likely, but it certainly was possible. Most people prefer the modest security of wearing underwear, but she was sure that there were those who enjoyed the freedom of being au natural.

Jessie's legs moved back and forth as she imagined her visitor getting out of bed. Beads of sweat dripped over his lean and muscular chest. He stretched out his arms trying to awaken his body. Tight mocha-colored skin covered large ropes of muscles in his legs, tightening even more as he prepared to stand up. Sinewy muscles in his upper back seemed to roll with his every movement. Jessie's eyes closed as she wrapped her arms around his bronzed body. He gently grabbed her and pulled her to him. As she rubbed her body against his, she could feel his manhood coming to life. It rose slowly up her leg to her torso. He made a quick maneuver that placed it between them and against her stomach. He slowly bent over and pressed his lips next to hers, his tongue darting in and out of her mouth. She kissed him hard running her tongue over his passion-swollen lips. Her hands ran frantically over his muscular back and tight buttock and as far down his legs as she could reach.

She broke free and took one step back. Slowly, she pulled the man's tee shirt she was wearing over her head and threw it on the floor. She was wearing no bra. He moaned as his eyes fell on her ample breasts as they heaved up and down in the morning sunlight. She slowly unbuttoned her shorts and let them fall to the floor. He muttered something aloud as he stared at the patch of blond hair between her legs. She glanced down at his huge penis. In spite of its enormous weight, it was standing straight out as if defying gravity. It bounced slightly as it throbbed with his racing heartbeat. Jessie dropped to her knees. She wrapped her hand around its girth, opened her mouth and...

"Morning."

Jessie jumped and spun around.

"Whoa," said Porter. "Where the hell were you?"

"What do you mean?" she asked trying to regain her composure.

"Your mind was someplace else. You didn't hear me until I said something."

"So?"

"So, I think your mind was on that bunkhouse."

"Why would I do that?"

Porter sipped his coffee and sat down beside her. "He's out there, isn't he?"

"What are you talking about?"

"You hired that nigger, didn't you?"

"How did you find out about that?"

"It's all over town, woman," he said at the top of his voice. "As if we don't have enough problems around here."

"Well, Spencer is here to fix one of our problems."

"Spencer is here to fix one of our problems?" said Porter in a mocking voice. "Spencer is now our biggest problem. Do you have any idea what could happen once the good old boys in this town hear about your Spencer?"

"Hey, that's why we have a sheriff in this town."

"Calvin Hicks? Good Lord, where have you been? Calvin is a member of the Klan. A lot of good he will be."

Jessie sipped her coffee. "I actually don't care. The boy needed a job, and I need a roof put on the barn. When he's done, he'll move on."

Porter frowned as he stared at Jessie's face. "You got the hots for him, don't you?"

"Don't be a jerk, Porter."

"Oh, my God! I can't believe it," said Porter. "You'll fuck a nigger, but you won't fuck me?"

"Aren't you getting a little carried away?" said Jessie. "I hired the man to put a new roof on the barn, and that's all."

"You know, everyone in town thinks of you as a slut. They talk about you all the time. I see them talking, and they go quiet when I get near them. I know what they're talking about. It's really no secret."

"That's enough, " said Jessie, her head bent and a lone tear streaking down her face.

"Don't you have any loyalty to dad? How do you think he's gonna feel when he gets back here and hears all the rumors?"

Suddenly, Jessie's humiliation turned to anger. "And what makes you think you're the perfect example of humanity? You're lazy and an alcoholic with no purpose in life other than collecting your inheritance. How does it feel to know that your father feels nothing but shame for you?"

Porter began to laugh. He laughed hysterically.

Jessie turned to him. "And what on earth is it that you find so funny about this?"

Porter soon regained his composure. He wiped a tear from his eye. "Think about it. The only virtuous one is Pop, and he ain't here because he's off someplace working to keep this place alive."

"I still don't get it," she said with a confused look on her face.

"He's working his ass off for two scumbags, both of whom are screwing everybody in town." He paused, and his face sobered. "Kinda gets ya right here, doesn't it?"

Jessie dumped the last of her coffee onto the ground. "God, you have a sick way of looking at things."

"Truth hurts."

Jessie got to her feet and started for the door. "I gotta get away from you."

"Fix me some breakfast," Porter yelled.

"Yeah, that'll happen," she said and closed the door behind her.

A short time later, there was a gentle tapping on the screen door. Jessie was leaning over the stove. She turned her head and shouted, "Come in."

The door screeched, and Spencer stepped inside.

She turned and glanced at her visitor. "Good morning, Spencer," she said returning to the skillet.

"Good morning, Mrs. Harlan," he said still standing in the doorway.

"I'm fixing us some bacon and eggs. There's coffee over there on the counter."

"Well, thank you very much, Mrs. Harlan. I appreciate it."

He walked over and poured himself a cup. He then stood with his back against the wall while he sipped his coffee.

Jessie picked up the skillet and slid eggs onto two different plates. She glanced at Spencer. "Have a seat. You weren't figuring on eating standing up, were you?"

"No, ma'am," he said pulling out a chair. "It's just that some folks don't take to my kind sitting at the same table with white people. Oh, they'll feed us alright, it's just that we got to sit with our own."

Jessie put strips of bacon and toast on the plates and set them on the table. "Dig in," she said.

Spencer pulled the plate in front of him. He then folded his hands, closed his eyes and mumbled a quick blessing. He opened his eyes to see Jessie staring at him with a shocked look on her face. "Sorry," he said forcing a humble smile.

"Oh, no. That's quite alright," she said. "It's just that I haven't seen anything like that in a long time."

Spencer took a bite of his bacon. "Your family doesn't believe in God?"

"Oh, I suppose we do," she said. "Just never talk about it." She paused. "Do you go to church and believe in that sort of thing?"

"Yes, ma'am, I sure do. Can't say as I remember a time I didn't."

"So you believe that some Being created all this including the universe and all."

"Oh, yes, ma'am."

Jessie took a bite of her eggs. "Don't you find it a bit hard to believe?"

"No disrespect, ma'am, but I ain't never heard anything better. They tell me there a group of people who say we came from the apes. If that were the case, why are there still apes? Another bunch says we came up from something that slithered out of the sea. I don't know about you, but I'd much rather think of myself as a creation rather than some mutant slug from the ocean."

Jessie laughed. "Well, you got a good point there." She paused, her face sobered. "You have to admit that believing in some Creator of the universe can be a challenge sometimes."

Spencer finished eating one of his eggs. "The way I figure it, He only made us with enough brains to survive here on earth. We just ain't smart enough to understand things beyond earth. That's why we have to have faith…faith in the good Lord."

Jessie grew quiet. For some reason that she couldn't understand, she felt uncomfortable with the conversation. She finished her meal and leaned back in her chair. "So, you come from Detroit."

"Yes, ma'am."

"I always thought that was a great place to live," she said. "What's so bad about Detroit to make you want to leave?"

"I just can't stand city living, I guess. I know that my kind usually lives in cities, but I just don't like it any more. I just have to see if small town life is better."

"A small town is one thing," said Jessie. "But Steam Corners is another. We aren't even big enough to be called a small town."

"Seems nice to me," he said sipping his coffee.

"You might change your mind after you get to know the people," said Jessie with a devilish smile.

Spencer said nothing.

"I ordered the materials you'll need for the roof," said Jessie. "They should be delivered later today."

"So, who do we have here?" said Porter stumbling into the kitchen.

Spencer jumped to his feet.

"Spencer, this is Porter," said Jessie with a sneer. "Porter, this is Spencer."

Spencer thrust his hand towards Porter.

"So, you gave my breakfast to this guy?" he said ignoring Spencer's gesture.

"I don't remember making you any breakfast in the first place," said Jessie.

"No fucking surprise there," said Porter. He opened the refrigerator and pulled out a bottle of beer.

Spencer sat back down.

"So, you're going to put a roof on our barn," said Porter opening the bottle. "Ever do any work like that?"

"Yes, sir."

Porter leaned against a kitchen cabinet. "You've put a roof on a barn?"

"No, sir. I've done roofing jobs on houses and chicken coops."

"I thought you said you had done a barn before."

"No, sir. You asked me if I had ever done any work like that."

Porter chugged his beer. "Shit, boy, putting a roof on a chicken coop is a hell of a lot different than doing a barn. Wait 'til your black ass is forty feet in the air. Tell me then all about barns and chicken coops."

"Give it a rest, Porter," said Jessie. "My God, you are rude."

"You call me rude? I didn't eat his fucking breakfast."

Jessie slowly shook her head. "Jesus, Porter."

"I hear you're from Detroit," said Porter gulping his beer. "You must know all about fighting and killing. I hear your people do that a lot up there. Can't get along, so you up and kill one another. Sounds great to me as long as you aren't killing white folks."

Spencer turned to Jessie. His jaw was tight, and his lips set in a straight line. He got to his feet. "I best be getting outside. I got some work to do."

Porter moved over blocking the doorway. "Maybe I ain't done talking to you," said Porter. "And maybe you work for us and will come and go when we say you will."

Spencer stopped in front of Porter. "Mr. Harlan, I got no fight with you. I just want to go work. That's all."

"Let him go, Porter," said Jessie. "We're not paying him to listen to your bullshit."

Porter slowly stepped aside.

It was after nine in the evening when Jessie finished work. She walked outside and breathed in the cool night air. She started for her car when she heard a voice from across the street.

"Jessie, how are you?"

The voice was coming from a car parked next to hers. She bent over to see inside the car. "Harrison, what are you doing here?"

"I…I just had to see you. How have you been?"

"Fine. Just fine. Everything alright with you?"

"I'm okay."

"What are you doing out here?"

"Well, I was wondering if you would go someplace to get a drink."

"It's kinda late, don't you think? Besides, Coonies is the only place around here."

"I suppose you're right," he said. "Would you mind stopping over at my place for a drink?"

Jessie said nothing.

"I promise one drink, and you're on your way."

She paused again.

"I just wanted to see you."

"Okay. One drink."

The cool night air felt good as she followed Harrison in his car. She could see his arm hanging out of the car ahead of her. Occasionally, she could see his outline from approaching headlights that lit up the inside of his car. He was a good man, an honest man. He was the kind of man her mother told her to marry. He wasn't rich, but chances were good that someday his job would make him that way.

He was interested in her, and she was attracted to him, but something was bothering her. She couldn't stop thinking about Spencer. She knew there was no future for the two of them. White women just didn't marry black men. That was unspeakable. She was nearly ten years older than he was. Chances were good that he regarded her as an old woman, someone with whom he would never have an interest. There were cultural differences between them. He was from the city, and she was from a dying small town. Actually, when she thought about it, he never showed even the slightest interest in her. Maybe if things were different. Maybe if she wasn't his boss, he might have tried something.

Harrison came to a stop in front of his house. She brought her car to a stop and ran her fingers through her hair. She needed to get that boy out of her head. After all, he was just a boy. Hell, if his birthday had been two months later, she wouldn't have been allowed to serve him beer. She glanced at Harrison as he got out of his car. She knew that if she were to have any kind of future, it would be with that man. She knew that was a fact, and she knew she had to get Spencer out of her mind.

Harrison stopped beside her car and opened the door. "Actually, I wanted to show you some of the improvements I've made and see what you think."

"I'd love to," she said getting out of her car.

Harrison opened the front door and stood aside to allow her a chance to view the living room.

Jessie surveyed the room. "Very nice," she muttered with a smile on her face.

Harrison beamed with pride after hearing her comment. "Thanks."

"The place doesn't look the same," she said still scanning the room. "It looks like a different house."

"What do you think of the curtains?"

"Very nice. They look…modern."

"Is that good?"

"Yes, that's very good."

"Had a time hanging them," he said. "They need to write those instructions for morons like me."

"How 'bout the other rooms?"

"Besides this room, the only other thing I've done is to unpack all my stuff and find a place for it. Until this, I never realized how many utensils one needs for cooking. Spent all my time rummaging through boxes."

"Well, if the lawyer business doesn't work out, you could always become a home decorator."

Harrison beamed as if he had just received an "A" on his homework. "Thanks again," he said pointing at the couch. "Have a seat, and I'll fix us a drink."

Jessie took a seat and listened to him frantically working in the kitchen. Moments later, he returned with a drink in each hand. He handed her one and then took his place at the other end of the sofa.

"Why are you sitting way down there?" she asked with a playful voice.

Harrison sipped his drink. "Well, I didn't want to give you the impression the other day I expected anything. You know…anything other than to talk to you."

"That's very sweet of you, Harrison."

Harrison paused as he thought about what to say. "I hear you have a new farm hand."

"News travels fast in a small town," she said with a note of sarcasm in her voice.

"Is it true what they say? Is he a black man?"

Jessie's smile disappeared. "Do you have a problem with that?"

"Oh, no. Not me. Actually, I think this seedy little town could use a shaking up. We need new blood. It's just that there are those who want to keep things the way they have always been."

"Harrison, you're too kind," said Jessie. "They're called bigots, plain and simple."

Some people just simply can't accept change," said Harrison.

"That's because they're backward hillbillies," she said, her voice angered.

Harrison forced a smile. "You like this guy, don't you?"

Jessie whipped her head around. "Why do you say that?"

"I don't know. I maybe reading something into it, but I somehow got that impression."

Jessie turned back to her drink. "So, what if I do?"

"I could see how a young lady's head would be turned. I hear he's quite handsome."

"He's okay looking."

"Someone said he's the quiet type."

Jessie smiled. "That he is. He's very quiet, kinda shy, and he's extremely polite. Says ma'am, thanks and all kinds of nice things. You don't see that around here much anymore."

Harrison gulped his drink and set the glass on the table. "You know, you get a little giddy when you talk about him. I think you're in love with this guy."

"I'm ten years older than Spencer. He wouldn't give me a second thought," she said her voice getting stronger and louder. "Besides, what business is that of yours?"

"Silly me," said Harrison with an angry voice. "I thought we had something going."

"The only thing we had going was a one night thing, and now I'm sorry that ever happened."

Harrison drained his glass and slammed it back on the table. "I'll bet you wouldn't regret a night with your precious Spencer."

Jessie jumped to her feet and stormed across the floor. She opened the front door and turned to Harrison. "You can go to hell, Harrison Benson. You're just one more asshole bigot in this town." With that, she slammed the door behind her.

Chapter Seven

It was late morning when the Johnson Lumber Company truck stopped in front of the Harlan barn. Lowell, the owner, grabbed his clipboard and jumped out of the truck. He marched up to the back porch and knocked on the door. He waited for a few moments and knocked again. He was just about ready to leave when the door slowly opened. Porter appeared dressed only in his underwear. His eyes were slits and his hair unkempt.

"Hey Porter," said Lowell. "Where's your mother?"

Porter began to scratch his groin. "She ain't my mother."

"Quit dickin' around, Porter. Where's Jessie?"

"I don't know. Is the truck out back?"

Lowell spun around. "Don't see it."

"She's gone to town then. Said something about needing groceries."

"Damn, I need someone to sign for this load. How 'bout you, Porter?"

"I ain't signing for shit."

Lowell turned to leave. "Tell Jessie it will probably be next week before I can get back out here."

Just then, the bunkhouse door opened and out stepped Spencer.

Porter stared at him then shouted at Lowell, "Come back here. I'll sign for it."

Lowell held out the clipboard, and Porter signed the paperwork. When he finished, he turned to Lowell and said, "Now, take that black bastard over there and get that shit unloaded." He then turned and went back inside.

It was nearly an hour later when they finished. Porter stepped outside. He slowly walked across the yard and stopped in front of Spencer who was busy unloading supplies.

"You don't have a clue of what you're doing, do you?" asked Porter.

Spencer stopped and stared at Porter. He said nothing and went back to work.

"Let me ask you something," said Porter stepping even closer. "How are you going to get all those materials up there on that roof?"

Spencer stopped and looked at Porter. "I plan to carry them up."

Porter laughed. "Do you seriously think you can carry all that up a ladder by yourself?"

"Yes, sir."

"No way in hell."

"Maybe for someone in your physical condition, but I'll be all right," said Spencer.

"Whoa. Hold on there. Was that a shot you gave me?"

"No, sir. Just stating a fact."

"You sure are a smart-ass, aren't you boy?"

Spencer said nothing. He bent over and started to work.

You know, you think you're pretty tough, but I could kick your ass any day," said Porter.

Spencer paused for a moment, smiled and went back to work.

"What are you smiling at, boy? I've a mind to kick your ass right now."

Spencer unbuttoned his shirt and hung it on a nail. Sweat glistened on his bronze muscular body. "Go back in the house, Mr. Harlan. I have work to do."

Porter stepped closer. "Big tough guy from Detroit."

Spencer stopped, his body was erect and his legs spread apart. "I'm warning you, Mr. Harlan."

Porter paused. There was something different about this man, something menacing. Porter was never much of a fighter. At least, he was never a fair fighter. He only fought smaller and weaker men and only if he could get the drop on them. Porter relaxed and stepped back.

"I'll let you go this time," said Porter. "After all, I want to watch you kill yourself putting on this roof."

Spencer relaxed as well. He said nothing but bent over to pick up a board. With one of his feet, Porter pushed Spencer over into the dirt. Spencer sprang to his feet and went into a fighting stance. "Mr. Harlan, if you ever touch me again, any way at all, I will retaliate."

Porter waved his hand as a dismissal. "Good Lord, boy, I was just havin' fun with you," he said, turned and started towards the house. "Get your ass back to work. You're wasting too much time."

It was nearly an hour later when Jessie pulled in the drive. She parked next to the back door and carried several bags of groceries into the house. Minutes later, she walked across the yard and stopped near the barn.

"Porter said you tried to pick a fight with him," she said with a smile and an attitude of indifference.

"That's not the way it happened," said Spencer.

"Don't worry," she said. "I always know when Porter is lying which is most of the time."

"He sure is a strange guy," said Spencer.

"I'm sure he was the guy who tried to pick a fight with you, wasn't he?"

"Yes, ma'am. He gave it a try."

"Why didn't you kick his ass? It's obvious that he would be no problem for you."

"I really didn't want to hurt him seeing as how he's kin to you. Besides, I got no beef with him. He's just a little mouthy."

"He might be my husband's son, but he ain't no kin to me. Next time he bothers you, go ahead and make him cry. I'd love to see it."

"Yes, ma'am, I sure will," he said with a forced smile.

There was a pause.

"Can I get you anything? Lemonade? Water?"

"If you don't mind, I've been drinking from the garden hose."

"That's fine," she said. "But if you change your mind, just let me know."

"I surely will, Mrs. Harlan."

"You know, I told you about that Mrs. Harlan business. You can call me Jessie if you want."

"Sorry, but I can't say as I can do that," he said.

"Why is that?"

"My daddy didn't teach me much, but he did tell me to respect my elders."

Jessie frowned. "I'm no elder to you."

"Beg pardon, ma'am, but you're considerable older than me."

"Maybe by a few years."

"If you say so, Mrs. Harlan."

Jessie laughed. "I'll leave you to your work. If you need anything, just let me know."

It was the middle of the afternoon. There wasn't a cloud in the sky, and the temperature was in the mid-nineties. Spencer had carried nearly all of the supplies to the top of the barn. His body was drenched in sweat, but he kept working as if he were unaffected by the strenuous work.

Jessie slipped out the back door with a glass of lemonade and sat on the porch swing. She gazed across the yard at the shirtless black man working on her barn. His shoulders, chest and arms glistened with sweat. As he picked up large pieces of lumber, his huge biceps flexed into peaks. She could see that his whole body was nothing more than ebony skin covering lean muscle from the bulging blood veins that scattered across his body.

Her lips slightly parted as she stared at the young man. She had been with a lot of men in her time, but she had never seen one quite like this one. She wondered if all black men looked like him without their shirts on. She then thought about Detroit and all the black men who lived there. Spencer had said there were thousands. She wondered if they all looked like him and if they would want her.

She turned her thoughts to Spencer. She had bragged all her life that she had never met a man who didn't desire her sooner or later. Some took a bit of seduction, but eventually, they all gave in, and, yet, here was this man who acted as if she were some ugly fat woman far older than he was. He obviously had more self-discipline than most. He would give in if she tried to seduce him. There was no doubt in her mind. No man could resist her. She could control any man if she wanted him, and Spencer was no different.

It seemed strange to her why she wanted him so bad. He was good looking and virile, but so were many other men in her life. Was it because he was black? Yes, that must be the reason. It was the forbidden fruit thing. She desired that which she was not allowed to have. And, yet, there was another possibility. For the first time, she had met a man who showed no signs of wanting her. Yes, that was definitely it. She couldn't stand the idea that a man could resist her. Here was one man who showed no signs of desire for her.

She had to get him alone. Maybe she could stop by the bunkhouse late one night while he was asleep. She would take off her clothes and get into bed with him. She was so confident in her charm that she would skip the seduction and go straight for the jugular. He would awaken to find her body pressed against his. She would kiss him hard running her tongue over his swollen lips. She would crawl up on top of him and gently drag her nipples across his chest. She would kiss all over his chest running her tongue down to his stomach and over his groin. By then he would be erect. There's no way he could stop that from happening. She would take it in her hand and run her tongue up one side and down the other, then thrust it in her mouth as far down as it would go.

He would undoubtedly belong to her by then. There was no question about it. But there was something better. Seduction was the essence of sex. It intensified the excitement, the anticipation of what was to come. She would slowly take off her clothes and hold her bare breasts just inches from his face giving him full instructions not to touch. She would see how tough he was. She would test his self-discipline, and he would lose.

"Mrs. Harlan," said Spencer standing over her.

She didn't respond.

"Mrs. Harlan," he said again.

She was staring across the field in a trance-like state.

"Mrs. Harlan," he shouted.

"Yes, Spencer," she said batting her eyes. "What do you need?"

"Sorry to bother you, Mrs. Harlan, but I was wondering if I could get a glass of that lemonade. The water from the hose is almost too hot to drink."

· She scrambled to her feet. "Sure Spencer," she said. "I'll be right back."

Spencer ran his hand over the porch railing. Peeling paint scattered everywhere.

"Here you go," said Jessie carrying a big glass of iced lemonade. "Have a seat."

Spencer sat on the edge of the porch and gulped his drink. "Your house needs to be painted."

Jessie took a quick glance at the porch. "It's needed it for a long time."

"I'll do it," said Spencer.

"Oh, I'd love to get it done, but I can't afford it."

"I'll do it for rent and board."

"Really?"

"You supply the paint, and I'll do the work."

Jessie paused. "I'll think about it."

Spencer sipped his drink. "Having second thoughts about housing a black guy?"

"Honey, if I had a problem like that, I wouldn't have hired you in the first place. Besides, I think it's good for this town."

"So hiring me was your way of getting your name on the lips of everyone in town."

"Hey, you were the one who needed a job," she said. "I just hired you. Don't make it out to more than that."

Spencer paused. "You're right. Sorry. Guess I was being a bit too sensitive."

"That's funny," said Jessie. "I've only known one other black person, and he was sensitive too. Seems no matter what I said he would screw it around to sound like I was prejudice. I gotta tell you, that got old real fast."

"Don't doubt it."

"Tell me, Spencer," said Jessie. "What's it like being a black person living in a world of white people?"

Spencer paused. He sipped his drink. "Imagine walking into a restaurant or a bar full of black people and you're the only white. Happens everyday." He gulped his drink and handed her the glass. "Thanks for the drink. Gotta get back to work."

Jessie watched as he walked away. "God, I want you," she muttered.

It was only moments later that a familiar car pulled into the driveway. It parked near the barn, and Harrison Benson got out. He was dressed in a suit and tie. He walked to the back porch and stood in front of Jessie.

"What do you want?" asked Jessie with an air of indignation.

"I came here to apologize," said Harrison. "May I sit down?"

Jessie nodded, and he pulled up a lawn chair.

Harrison took a deep breath. "I said things I shouldn't have, and for that I'm sorry."

"Is that it?"

"No, not really," he said and paused. "I realized how much you mean to me. I think I'm in love with you."

"May I point out to you that I'm a married woman."

"I know all that," he said. "But I can't help my feelings. The minute I said those ugly things I regretted it. I soon realized that it's bad enough that you're a married woman, but to have you mad at me is even worse. There's nothing I can do about the fact that you're married, but I can make things right between you and me."

Jessie said nothing. She slowly rocked the swing back and forth. Finally, a tiny smile appeared on her face. "I should make you grovel at my feet."

Harrison smiled. "Hey, I'm good at groveling. I'm a lawyer, don't forget."

"I could have had you wash my car, you know."

"You want your car washed? I'll do it. After all, I should be washing cars for a living. There's gotta be more money in it."

Jessie laughed. "Wanna come inside for a cup of lemonade?"

"Sure," he said and followed her through the back door.

It was over an hour later that the back door swung open. Harrison stepped out on the porch carrying his suit coat and tie. Jessie followed wearing a different pair of shorts and a tee shirt with no bra. She stumbled across the porch like she had been drinking. She walked with him across the yard to his car. Spencer was standing nearby wiping his hands with a damp cloth.

"So you're the new hired hand around here," said Harrison extending his hand.

"Call me Spencer," he said taking his hand.

"I'm Harrison Benson," he said. "I gotta envy you."

"How's that, sir?"

"You get to live right here with this beautiful woman."

"You're right about that, sir. That's a fact."

Harrison turned to the barn. "How's it going?"

Spencer looked at the top of the barn. "Very well, sir. Hope to get 'er finished before we get any bad weather."

"Not much chance of that," said Harrison, his smile disappearing. "It's been a long time since we've seen even a sprinkle."

"Okay, Mr. Benson," said Jessie. "My help can't anything done with the likes of you jawing with him."

Harrison turned back to Spencer. "Nice meeting you."

"Nice meeting you, sir," he replied.

Harrison got in his car and started the engine. "I'll take care of that legal matter for you, Mrs. Harlan," he said in an effort to disguise the purpose of his visit.

Jessie smiled as he drove away.

She turned to Spencer with a playful look on her face. "I may have been drinking, but I still caught you looking," she said slowly prancing in a small circle.

"Ma'am?"

"You were peeking at my chest, weren't you? You can see right through this shirt, can't you?"

"No, ma'am," he said with a sober face. "That would be disrespectful."

"Disrespectful? What does that have to do with anything? You're a man. If you get a chance to see a white woman's breasts, you take it. Am I not right?"

"It wouldn't be right for me to…"

"Oh, you're right about that," she said. "A black man looking at a white woman's breasts. That ain't right. Men have been killed for less. Kinda makes it all the more tempting, doesn't it? Kinda like the forbidden fruit thing."

"Why are you talking like this, Mrs. Harlan?" Spencer asked. "You and I have had nothing but a business relationship. I don't want any trouble."

"There's no trouble at all," she said fidgeting with the bottom of her shirt. "Besides, you started it. Yes, indeed. You were the one who was peeking at my chest. I'll bet you could see the dark nipples through my shirt. Is that what you saw? Can't blame you. It's only natural for any man to want to see a woman's breasts."

Spencer started to turn away. "I gotta get back to…"

"Hey, work can wait," she said and grasped the bottom of her shirt with both hands.

He turned back to face her.

"Wanna see these babies or not?"

"Mrs. Harlan, I don't think…"

She pulled up the shirt just enough to reveal her flat stomach. "Say the word, and the shirt comes off."

Spencer glanced at her chest and then returned to her face. "It ain't right, Mrs. Harlan. It just ain't right."

"Nobody is going to know about this. It will be between you and me. What harm can come of that?"

"I don't think…"

"Unless, of course, you don't want to see them," she said with a scowl. "Is that it? You don't care to see them?"

"Oh, I don't think…"

"Good God! I never thought about this before, but I got you over a barrel. If you say you want to see them, that means you desire a white woman. If you say that you don't want to see them, that's a direct insult. You're saying I'm not pretty enough. Back's against the wall, ain't it, Spencer? Damned if you do, damned if you don't. What are ya gonna do now?"

Spencer stepped back until he was against the side of the barn. Jessie closed the gap until she was nearly pressed against him. His eyes were wandering elsewhere. "Look at me!" she commanded. He bowed his head and focused on her eyes. With one swift movement, she pulled her shirt over her head and threw it on the ground. His eyes remained fixed on hers. "Look at them!" she shouted. He didn't move. Sweat poured down his face. She grabbed one of his hands and placed it on her breast. She smiled as he glanced at her chest. He held it there for a moment, then pulled it away. "Firm, ain't they?" She then moved closer until her breasts pressed into his bare stomach. "These could be laying on your chest if you want," she said with a heavy voice. "We can do it right here in the bunkhouse or in my bedroom. Just say the word."

Spencer gently broke free. He turned and started for the bunkhouse.

"I don't believe it," she said with an indignant voice. "I simply don't believe it. You have the perfect opportunity to fuck a white woman, and you walk away. Well, you blew it. That was your big chance, and you blew it. There ain't a man in town who would turn me down, but you did. You'll regret this day, Mr. Perfect. You'll live to regret this day."

Chapter Eight

The next morning started as they all did with a hot morning sun and the promise of it getting even hotter. Spencer stepped out of the bunkhouse and stared at the unfinished roof on the barn. He turned to the house. Jessie had been waiting on the front porch and was already walking towards him. After yesterday's encounter, he had hoped to avoid her. He wasn't quite sure how to do it, but he was certain that it would, at the very least, be uncomfortable.

"Don't remember much about yesterday, but I know enough that I owe you an apology."

"That's okay, Mrs. Harlan."

"Me and alcohol never did mix all that good," she said folding her arms over her chest. "Hope you'll forgive me."

"No harm done," he said with a polite smile.

"You said something about needing some nails," she said handing him some money. "I got one massive headache. Take this and go into town. You can get your nails at Bailey's Hardware."

Spencer took the money. "Thanks. Be back as soon as I can"

It was a short trip to town, less than two miles. It was early, and the town was quiet. He parked in front of the hardware store and stepped inside. He scanned the room and saw that the nails were on a counter nearby. He was partially hidden from the rest of the store but could hear disturbing conversation coming from the next aisle.

Red Harris had been considered the town bully since he was old enough to walk. He had stopped in the hardware with no intention of buying anything, discovered an eighteen-year-old black girl and proceeded to humiliate her as he always did. Red was trying to convince her to go home with him, and of course she was resisting. Red was holding her preventing her from leaving when Spencer stepped around the corner.

"Let her go," Spencer commanded.

Still holding the young girl, Red turned to find Spencer standing in front of him. "So this is the new nigger in town. You're the one staying out at the Harlan's, aren't you?"

"I said let her go."

Red forced a nervous laugh. "I hear you're from Detroit. That would explain your bad manners."

Spencer dropped to a fighting stance.

"Whoa, what the fuck is that?" said Red.

"I won't warn you again. Let her go, or I will force you to do so."

Red eased his grip on the girl, and she moved away. "Hey, don't get all riled up," said Red. "I was just having a little fun."

Howard Bailey was the owner of the store and stepped into the aisle. "Go on, Red, and get the hell out of here. That boy looks as if he could kick your ass from here to Dublin." They all watched as Red walked out of the building. Howard turned to Spencer and the girl. "Sorry about that. Red has the brains of a chipmunk. All we can hope is that someday he'll drown in his own spit."

Spencer stepped over to the girl. "Are you okay?"

"I'm okay," she said her voice still shaky. She picked up the small bag she was carrying. "Thanks for helping me out."

"Glad to do it. My name is Spencer," he said offering his hand.

"Skeeter is my name," she said lightly shaking his hand.

"Let me pay for my nails, and I'll walk you outside," he said and without waiting for an answer disappeared around the corner. Moments later, he rejoined her and led her to the front door.

"Pretty classy guy you were hooked up with," said Spencer with a smile.

"I was told to avoid Red Harris, and now I know why."

Spencer opened the screen door to let her out and closed it behind him. "Pardon me for saying so, but I thought I was the only non-white in this town," said Spencer.

"Oh, this town has gone to hell, if you will excuse the bad word. Not only is there you and me but my mama as well."

Well, that settles it," said Spencer with a smile. "I wouldn't want to live in a town that would allow the likes of me. Lose all respect for it."

"You're funny," said Skeeter walking at a fast pace.

Spencer picked up the pace. "Where are you going in such a hurry?"

"Home."

"Where do you live?"

"On the other side of town."

"Want me to drive you? Ain't much of a car, but it beats walking."

"No, thanks."

"Why not?"

"I don't know you. I just met you."

"I just saved you from that redneck Harris."

"That doesn't mean you aren't some pervert or a deviate," she said with a smile. "In fact, if I was to come upon you on the street, I'd probably cross over to avoid you."

"You think I look like some kind of pervert?" he asked still trying to keep up. "Come to think about it, I'm not all that sure what a pervert looks like. What does a pervert look like?"

Skeeter stopped only for a moment. "Look into a mirror," she said still smiling and resumed her walk.

Spencer was now running backwards in front of her. "So let me get this straight. I save you from certain disaster, and I'm a pervert. Have I got that right?"

"Exactly."

"Just for that, I think you should go with me to the barn dance on Saturday night."

"I don't think so."

"Why not?"

"I told you. I don't know you."

"Bring your mother along as a chaperon."

"Oh, and expose her to a pervert? I don't think so."

"How 'bout I ask your mother if it's okay?"

"You leave my mother out of this," she said and came to a stop. "Let me ask you something. Why on earth would a black man from Detroit want to go to a barn dance?"

"I don't."

"Then why are you asking me to go?"

"Would you go any place else with me?"

"No."

Spencer held out his hands. "Well, then. I can wear a plaid shirt and a cowboy hat. Stick chew in my mouth, and I can be the best nigger redneck you ever did see."

Skeeter tried to maintain her composure but started to laugh. "Pick me up at seven, and forget that chew business. Can't stand the smell."

Spencer only worked a half of a day on Saturday. He took his first week's pay and headed downtown to buy a new pair of jeans. He'd never been to a barn dance, and he wasn't quite sure what to wear, but he was fairly confident that there would be someone else wearing them.

He grabbed his package and walked outside. As he approached his car, he noticed four men leaning against it. One of them was Red Harris.

"Hey there, tough guy," said Red. "I haven't forgotten about the other day."

"Get off the car," commanded Spencer.

Red paused, then turned to the others and nodded. They slowly moved away from the car. "I wanted to show my friends here that fancy fighting stance you got. Do that again for me, will ya?"

"I got no beef with you, Mr. Harris," said Spencer. "Why don't you just leave me alone?"

"You damn sure were ready to fight the other day. What the hell happened? You aren't scared of my friends here, are you?"

"Mr. Harris, I'm neither scared of you or your friends. I just don't want this to go any further. Someone is going to get hurt. There may be many who might get hurt, even myself. The only thing I can be sure of is, you will get hurt, Mr. Harris."

Red doubled his fists. "You sound pretty tough, now let's see what you got."

The four men began to slowly circle Spencer. They slowly closed the circle and were about to attack when an extremely large black woman stepped off the curb.

"Red Harris, you and those idiot friends of yours leave that boy alone."

"You stay out of this, Tilly," said Red still in a fighting posture.

"If you don't leave him alone, I'll tell your mother on you, now git."

Red said nothing.

Tilly bent over and picked up a stick. "Damn yer nasty ass," she said and cracked the stick across Red's back. "Git yer white ass outta here."

"Damn, Tilly, that hurt," said Red.

"If you don't leave right now, I'm a gonna sit on you. And you know I'll do it."

Red paused. He turned and looked at the angry black woman. "C'mon boys. Let's get out of here."

Tilly stood guard as they slowly walked away. "And there was too much racket comin' from yer house last night while we were sleepin'. Knock that shit off," she said waving a finger at Red.

Tilly slowly shook her head. "Worst thing that ever happened to me was movin' in next to that brain dead dumb ass."

"Thanks for the help," said Spencer sticking out his hand. "My name is Spencer."

Tilly walked past Spencer ignoring his gesture. "Yeah, I know who you are. Everybody in town knows who you are, and if you do anything to my Skeeter tonight, the whole town will be comin' to yer funeral."

"Oh, so you're Skeeter's mother," said Spencer.

"Damn, you picked up on that so quickly. You ain't retarded, are ya?"

"No, ma'am."

"Well, you act like it."

"In all fairness, how was I to know?"

"There's three black folk a livin' in this town. There be you, and you already know Skeeter. So, who does that leave? You knew she was livin' with her mother. Damn, boy! All the clues were right there in front of ya, unless you be retarded."

Spencer withdrew his hand; his face sobered. "Sorry."

"Not half as sorry as yer gonna be if you try anything with my little girl. Hell, what are you doin' messin' around with a girl her age anyways? She's just a baby."

"All I want to do is to take her to the…"

"Don't tell me shit like that, you dummy. I knows what you want to do with my little girl. Damn, you are retarded."

"It's nothing like that," said Spencer with a frantic voice. "All we're going to do is to…"

Tilly stepped over to Spencer, grabbed a handful of his shirt and looked him in the eyes. "This is the last time I'm a gonna say this. If you so much as touch my little girl, you'll be a peeing sittin' down for the rest of yer life. Got it?"

"Yes, ma'am. I got it."

She released his shirt and pushed him away. "Now go get cleaned up. You'd better be spic and span when you come for my girl."

"Yes, ma'am," he said and backed away.

"And if you're as much as two minutes late, the deal's off. Can't stand for any man being late. Means you ain't learned no manners...unless, of course, you're retarded. And the jury is out on you."

It was nearly 6:30 when Spencer stepped out of the bunkhouse. He was wearing his new jeans and a fresh, clean shirt. He was strutting across the yard towards his car when Jessie stopped him. She glanced down at his feet.

"You're wearing cowboy boots," she said with a sneer on her face. "Never seen one of your kind wearing cowboy boots. Must be you're going to something really special."

Spencer said nothing. He could see empty beer bottle lying in the yard by the porch.

"So, you're taking out Tilly's little girl, huh? Planning on getting any?"

Spencer remained silent.

"She's a cute little thing. Bet she'd be a good fuck. Don't you think?"

"Mrs. Harlan, all I want to do is to..."

"Oh, I know what you want to do. You're no different than any other man. You're all the same. Tell a woman anything just to get what you want. 'Cept you. You're different. Ain't quite figured you out yet. Either you're one of them funny guys who likes other men, or maybe...yeah, maybe you think you're better than me."

"Mrs. Harlan…"

"Yeah, that's it. Why else would you turn me down? I've done everything but rub it in your face," she said then gestured for him to leave. "Go on and get out of here. Go to that little black bitch. I don't need you anyhow. I can have any man in town. Why the hell would I want a nigger like you?"

Spencer quickly got in his car and drove off. As he pulled onto the road, she was, by then, screaming obscenities and staggering through the cloud of dust left behind by his vehicle.

Spencer parked his car in front of Skeeter's house with ten minutes to spare. He got out of his car and bounced on her front porch. Before he could knock, Skeeter opened the screen door.

"Come on in," she said with a smile. "I want you to meet someone. Mother," she called out.

Tilly slowly stepped into the living room from the kitchen. She was wearing an apron and was carrying a butcher knife.

"I want you to meet my mother," she said.

The smile on Spencer's face disappeared. "We've met," he said.

"You've met my mother?"

"We met downtown earlier today," said Tilly.

"Well, that's nice," said Skeeter. "I wondered why you didn't want to give him the third degree."

"We already had a talk, didn't we, boy?"

"Yes, we did," said Spencer forcing a grin.

"You probably haven't forgot a word of it, have you, boy?"

"Etched in my head."

"Well, you kids go on now and have a good time," she said. "You have her home by eleven, you hear me?"

"Yes, ma'am. Eleven o'clock it is."

As Skeeter opened the front screen door, Spencer glanced at Tilly. She held the butcher knife in the air and pointed at it. She then pointed at his crotch with the knife. Spencer nearly ran out the door.

It was a hot summer evening. The sun was just beginning to set giving hope for even the slightest cool down. Spencer parked near a long row of other vehicles, and they started up a straw-covered path to the barn.

"Ever been to one of these things before?" asked Spencer.

"Are you kidding?"

"Has any black person been to one of these things?"

"We might be the first."

"Do they allow black folk in one of these things?"

"They probably never had to deal with such a problem," said Skeeter. "After all, what self-respecting black person would go to a barn dance?"

Spencer stopped. "Then why are we going?"

"I don't know."

"Know anyplace we could get a bite to eat?"

"There's a diner over on Route 39."

"What about your mother?" asked Spencer. "She's going to know we didn't go to the dance, and she's going to wonder where we went."

"The owner of the diner goes to our church," she said. "He'll vouch for us."

"Then, let's go," said Spencer.

It was a short drive to the other side of town. Since everyone in town was at the barn dance, the diner was all but empty. They found a booth near the back and ordered drinks.

"Your mother is one of a kind, thank God," said Spencer.

"She isn't bashful," said Skeeter. "You always know where you stand with her."

"That's for sure."

"Some people find that a bit unnerving. What do you think?"

"I like her honesty and candor. There is no confusion as to what's on her mind."

"I don't think I believe you."

"Oh, but it's true. Is there any doubt what time I'm suppose to bring you home tonight? No confusion at all."

"I hear you're from Detroit. What are you doing in a small town like Steam Corners?"

"Starting over, I guess. Had to get out of that town though. No place for man nor beast."

"It can't be all that bad," said Skeeter.

"Oh, yes it can."

"Your voice sounds so dramatic," said Skeeter. "Could it be we're exaggerating a bit?"

Spencer's face went cold. "No, I don't think so."

"Tell me. What could possibly happened to you to make you so bitter about that town?"

"Well, there were many things that happened to me, but I guess the last straw was watching my brother die in my arms from a gunshot wound."

"Oh, my God! What happened?"

There was a robbery of a drug store. My brother just happened to get in the way."

"That's terrible."

"They never did find the killer. Of course, they rarely do seeing as how it was a black boy who got killed.

"I can't believe it," said Skeeter holding her hand over her mouth.

"Funny thing was it never even made the news. Black people get killed up there all the time. Ain't no big deal."

"I'm so sorry."

"Well, now you know my story," said Spencer. I'll do anything to stay away from that place. Hell, I'll even wear a plaid shirt and these painful cowboy boots. The one thing I got going for myself is they can't call me a redneck."

Skeeter laughed. His joke helped break the tension.

"So, what about you?" Spencer asked. "What are you doing in place like this?"

"Well, I go where mama goes, and she goes where Mr. Benson goes."

"He's the new lawyer in town. Right?"

"That's him."

"Can't believe a little town like this could send enough business his way."

"Always pays mama on time," said Skeeter. Truth be known, she would work for nothing. She loves that man so much."

"There must be a reason," said Spencer.

"What's that?"

"There has to be a reason that your mama loves Mr. Benson," said Spencer. "My guess is she don't pass out her love to just anybody."

"It happened years ago," said Skeeter. "My Grandmother, Aggie, lived in a shack down by the railroad tracks. One day, a group of white boys was beating up a black boy right outside her place in her front yard. Grandma knew she should stay out of it. Lord knows what a bunch of bloodthirsty boys would do once they got the scent of blood. She tried to leave it alone, but she just couldn't. It didn't take any time at all before they turned on her. Imagine. A pack of boys beating up a ninety year old woman. When I think back on it, I still can't believe it. Any ways, it was about that time that Mr. Benson just happened to be driving by. He could have kept on going, but he didn't. Nobody would have known one way or the other, but that Mr. Benson stopped to help my Grandmother. He took one of the worst beatings anybody ever saw, but my grandmother got away. Hadn't been for him, she'd a most certainly been killed."

"I see now why your mama loves him," said Spencer.

"My mama loves or hates for keeps. There's no in between."

"Wonder how she feels about me?"

"We're on a date, aren't we?"

"Yeah."

"Trust me. She wouldn't have even let you on the front porch if she hated you."

"Somehow, I believe you," said Spencer. "That's one woman I would never butt heads with."

Skeeter shifted her weight in the booth. "I'm hungry. Let's order some food."

They both ate dinner and then talked some more. It was nearly 10:30 when Spencer glanced at the time.

"Oh, Good God, look at the time," he said. "I had no idea."

Skeeter smiled. "Worried about mama?"

Spencer got to his feet. "I'm worried about me if I don't get you home on time."

It was an even quicker trip across town. Spencer parked at the curb with ten minutes to spare. He glanced at the house and could see Tilly's outline in the living room window. He opened the door for Skeeter and walked her to her front door.

"I had a great time," said Skeeter. "Can't believe we talked that long." ·

"Most people can't get two words out of me, and I swear I talked the whole night."

There was a pause. It was an uncomfortable pause as Spencer stepped closer to Skeeter. He was nearly face-to-face with her when suddenly a voice from inside the house boomed out, "You earned one good night kiss, but in order to collect it, you must hold both of your hands behind your back."

Spencer looked at the window as if he could see Tilly. "Huh?" he said.

"You heard me right," said Tilly. "Put them hands of yours behind your back if you want that kiss."

Spencer hid his hands behind his back and leaned forward. Skeeter lightly placed a kiss on his cheek and withdrew.

"Alright, you're all through," said Tilly. "Now get on out of here."

He turned back to Skeeter. "Night, Skeeter," he said with a smile.

"Good night," she said and disappeared inside the house.

Spencer enjoyed the short trip back home. His mind played out the evening's events bringing a smile to his face for the entire trip. He turned off the road and parked his car by the barn. As he got out of his car, he glanced at the house. He could see the silhouette of Jessie sitting on the porch swing. He could see her drink from a bottle and throw it in the yard. It rolled a few feet and bumped into another empty bottle. Spencer hurried to the bunkhouse and closed the door behind him. He seemed relatively safe inside the bunkhouse. Nobody had ever been there, not even Jessie.

He sat on the edge of his cot and thought about the kiss from Skeeter. It seemed so innocent, almost a childlike experience. He smiled as he thought about Skeeter. He liked her. He liked her very much. And Tilly. What a woman. He liked her too in spite of her gruff exterior. He bent over and pulled off his boots. It felt great to get out of them.

He was just about to pull off his shirt when the bunkhouse door opened. It was Jessie. She stumbled inside dropping a nearly full bottle of beer onto the floor.

"So, how did it go?" she asked with an evil voice.

Spencer jumped to his feet. "What are you doing in here?" he asked.

"I don't know. I was under the impression that I owned this place."

"That still doesn't give you the right to come barging in here."

"Why? Were you afraid I was going to see you naked? 'Fraid I'd see that big black cock of yours?"

"You're drunk," said Spencer. "Why don't you go back to the house?"

"I just stopped out here to see how your date went."

"It was fine. We had a good time."

"Did you fuck her?"

"Go back to the house."

"Oh, you didn't get any, did ya?" said Jessie. "I'm really surprised. I thought that little black bitch would have been on her back in no time."

"Mrs. Harlan, nothing good is going to come of this."

Jessie leaned against Spencer with her arms on his shoulders. "That ain't right what she did to you. You must be horny. I mean when's the last time you ever had a woman? You went over there expecting to get laid, and she turned you down. That just ain't right. You must want someone really bad right about now. You'd probably settle for just about any woman. Right?" Jessie wrapped her hands around his neck and pulled his head down to hers. She quickly kissed his lips before he broke away. "C'mon. You'd even settle for me."

"Mrs. Harlan, this isn't going to happen."

"Oh, yes it is. If you want to keep your job, you're going to fuck me right here and now." She reached down and with one smooth motion pulled off her tee shirt. Her large breasts swayed as she did.

Spencer stepped back.

Jessie made her hands into fists and slammed them on her hips. "What the hell is wrong with you, boy? Are you queer or something? You're looking at the best fuck in town, and you turn it down?" She reached for his belt buckle and fumbled with it trying desperately to loosen it. Sweat poured from Spencer's face as he tried to fend off her attack.

"Alright, you son-of-a-bitch, I'm tired of fooling around," she said and began hitting him with her fists. Spencer covered his face and blocked as many of the punches as he could. With her long fingernails, she dug deep into his chest and arms then pulled down leaving tracks of blood behind.

Spencer pushed back her arms, then pushed her away.

She rushed back at him. There was blood in her eyes. "I'll kill you, you black bastard," she shouted and began to pound Spencer with closed fists. He blocked as many punches as he could, then grabbed her arms and pinned them to her body. With his other hand he forced her to the door and pushed her outside. Amazingly, she regained her footing to avoid falling down. She started back towards the bunkhouse. "You haven't heard the last of this, you bastard. You can't touch a white woman like that. You'll pay for that, you son-of-a-bitch. I'll tell everyone how you tried to rape me and guess what. You'll never see the courtroom. They'll get 'cha. Yes, they will. People around here don't hold with a black man raping a white woman. Ain't no jail big enough or strong enough to keep 'em out. They'll get 'cha."

Just as she stepped upon the porch, Spencer closed the door. He turned the lock and thrust the back of a chair under the knob. For the next few minutes, she rattled the door and screamed obscenities. Out of breath and tired, she turned and started for the house.

Once inside, she staggered across the kitchen to the sink. She leaned on the counter with her elbows nearly passing out from the alcohol. After a moment's rest, she glanced down.

"Oh, dear God," she muttered. "I forgot my shirt." She turned and faced the door, slightly losing her balance and falling back against the counter. "That son-of-a-bitch stole my shirt!" She opened a drawer and pulled out a butcher knife. She smiled as she held it in her hand. "It's time for you to get off my property, boy. You need to find a new job."

She started across the floor when the door opened.

Porter staggered in and closed the door behind him. "Good Lord, what do we have here?" he said with a smile. Jessie stopped and stood upright, her breasts exposed to the overhead light. "Oh, my God!" said Porter, his mouth gaping. "They're even better than I imagined."

"Stay away from me, Porter," said Jessie backing up against the counter.

"C'mon, let me feel one of them, honey. I promise I won't hurt nothing."

"You're messin' with the wrong person, Porter," she said her head still weaving. "I'm on my way to kill that nigger out there in the bunkhouse."

"Whoa, what do you want to go and do something like that for?"

"He wouldn't fuck me, Porter," she said her eyes now slits. "The son-of-a-bitch turned down a white woman. I ain't taking that from no man. No, sir."

"Well, now, ain't that a shame? I feel bad for you, honey. What you need is some good lovin' to forget all your problems. Now come on over here," he said, his arms spread wide.

"Get away from me, Porter. I ain't kiddin'."

Porter slowly stepped towards her. "Hey, we're both drunk. Let's take care of business and sleep it off. Things will look much better in the morning."

Jessie tightly gripped the knife and held it out in front of her. "Get out of my way."

Porter stepped closer. "Come to papa," he said with a grazed smile. "That bad black man was mean. Let me make it up to you."

"I'm warning you, Porter."

"You can warn me all you want, but you're giving it up this time. You can't keep teasing me like that and get away with it. I'm taking what's rightfully mine."

Jessie repeatedly thrust the knife in front of her as a warning. "Stay away from me, Porter. I'm on my way to that bunkhouse, and if you get in my way, I'll kill you as well. Don't matter to me. Never did like you anyhow."

Porter paused. "Oh, how could you say such a thing?"

"Hated you from the first day I met you. Never said anything out of respect for your dad."

"What did I ever do to you?"

"You're arrogant, lazy, and totally disrespectful to your dad and me."

Porter laughed. "Oh, but that's where you're wrong," he said taking a step closer. "I got all the respect in the world for you. I'm going to show you some of that respect right now."

Jessie tried to back up but her back was against the kitchen cabinet. She turned and slowly backed up against the wall.

"Ain't no place for you to go now," said Porter slowly creeping towards her. "Might as well give up."

Jessie stabbed at the air with the knife.

"Oh, that's so cute," said Porter. "But you're not even holding the knife right. Here let me show you."

Jessie glanced down at the knife in her hand. When she did, Porter lunged at her. Without thinking, she thrust the knife at him. It entered his lower chest and buried deep into his body. She glanced down. Only the handle was showing. Instinctively, she pulled it back out. Blood squirted like a geyser. It shot on her clothes and all over the floor.

Porter stood upright for a moment. He clutched at his wound with both hands trying to stop the bleeding. His face turned pale white. His eyes became slits. "What did you do to me?" he muttered.

Jessie began to sob. "I'm sorry, Porter. I didn't mean to do it. I don't know what happened."

Porter stumbled backward hitting the wall. A clock fell to the floor. "I need help," he muttered. "I need help now."

Blood pulsed from his wound in time to his fading heartbeat. Jessie stepped back. His eyes rolled to white, and he collapsed onto the floor. Jessie dropped the knife and stared in horror. He squirmed on the floor only for a moment then began to twitch.

Seconds later, his body seemed to relax and go still. She heard a final gasp for air then a subtle hissing of escaping air.

Jessie was in shock. She stood in the same spot motionless for what seemed like hours. Thick, red blood poured onto the floor deepening the pool and spreading it across the linoleum-covered floor. Jessie bent over and nudged the body. There was no response. She rolled him over onto his back, and the blood stop pouring from his wound.

She glanced at his face. "Oh, my God," she muttered. His mouth was slightly open and his eyes were glazed and staring at her. She jumped to her feet. It was if he were still alive. She moved to his other side. It was as if the eyes followed her. She kicked him in the back to confirm his demise. His eyes remained motionless.

Jessie pulled out a kitchen chair and sat down. "Oh, my God, what am I going to do?" she muttered. Surely they'll understand that it was an accident. Probably will never go to trial. After all, accidents happen. After the sheriff sees what happened, that will be the end of it all. Yet, how could she possibly say that it was an accident? Thrusting a knife into another person's chest would never be considered an accident. That will never work. But then again, why should she lie? Porter was trying to rape her. Yeah, that's my defense. He was trying to rape me, and I was only defending myself. Why not? After all, it was the truth. He was trying to rape her. He was drunk and was trying to rape her. The jury would believe her. They always take sides with the woman. Hell, people will probably applaud her for defending herself as well as the rights of all women. She quite possibly could become a hero from all this.

But what about Spencer? There must be a way to implicate him into all this. But that's impossible. He wasn't even in the house. In fact, he was probably asleep through the whole thing. Too bad she couldn't think of a way to pin this thing on him. It would serve him right. He thinks he's so high and mighty.

Wonder how big he'd feel when the sheriff would handcuff him and haul him away.

Jessie leaned back in her chair. She batted her eyes and shook her head. The rush of events seemed to sober her up. "There has to be a way," she said aloud. It was the perfect opportunity. She had a murdered body and a black man out in the bunkhouse. After all, why should she go through an investigation? Why should she go through the humiliation of a trial and people pointing at her wondering if she did it or not? Obviously, he would deny it. He would say that he had nothing to do with it. Most likely, he would point his finger at her and say that she did it. Of course, it would come down to his word against hers, and who is going to believe a black boy from the city over an innocent woman who had lived here all her life?

Jessie ran her fingers through her hair, and then it came to her. "That's it!" she shouted, then pointed at Porter's dead body. "It wasn't you who tried to rape me, it was that black boy out there in the bunkhouse. All you ever did was to try and defend me. Poor old Porter. You come home to find that evil black man trying to rape me, and you tried to stop him." She smiled. "How ironic. A rape charge for Mr. High and Mighty. He'll soon learn a lesson on pissing off a woman."

Jessie picked the knife off the floor. She wiped off the fingerprints and carried it outside. She walked over to the side of the bunkhouse and threw it behind the building. In the still night air, she could hear it as it landed in the tall weeds. By that time, the blood on her arms and hands had partially dried. She walked over to the garden hose and rinsed herself off carefully leaving traces of blood on the ground.

It was nearly 3:00 a.m. when his phone shattered the quiet. An overweight, middle-aged man rolled over in his bed and picked up the receiver. Before he could mutter a hello, a frantic voice came over the phone identifying herself as Jessie Harlan.

She was crying and saying something about a murder. He muttered that he would be right there and hung up the phone.

Calvin P. Hicks had been the sheriff of Douglas County for over thirty years. It was always a foregone conclusion that he would win re-election every time no matter who would dare run against him. It wasn't that he was all that great as an officer of the law, it was more that people knew him and felt safe having him around.

Since Steam Corners was a small village, they couldn't afford their own marshal, so they depended on Sheriff Hicks to protect them and enforce the law. Since Calvin had been born in Steam Corners, he considered it his privilege to help wherever possible.

Calvin swung his legs around and planted his feet on the floor. He picked up the phone again and placed a call. It rang twice before someone picked up.

"Bert, are you awake?"

"Who is this?"

"It's Calvin. Who did you think it was?"

"Jesus Christ, Cal. It's three in the morning."

"Get dressed and meet me at the Harlan farm."

"Bull shit, Calvin. I ain't a gonna do no such thing."

"You're an officer of the law, Bert. You're my deputy."

"I'm a nine to five deputy, Calvin. You don't pay me enough to get out of bed at three in the morning."

"Be there in fifteen minutes," he said and hung up the phone.

Calvin glanced down at his protruding stomach. He patted it with one hand and tried to suck it in.

It was only a five-minute drive to the Harlan farm. Bert's pickup truck was already there. Calvin got out of the cruiser and walked over to his deputy who was leaning against the fender of his truck.

"For God's sakes, Calvin, what's this all about?"

Calvin glanced down at his belly and smacked it with his hand. "Does it look like I've gained a few pounds? You can be honest with me. Really. I can take it."

"Jesus, Calvin. You've always been fat. I've never known you but what you weren't."

Calvin paused still clutching his stomach. "You don't have to be that honest."

"Well you asked for it."

Calvin patted his stomach again. "I just don't remember my gut being quite this big. I need to lay off those hamburgers down at the diner."

"Alright, Calvin," said Bert. "What are we doing over here at this time of the morning?"

Calvin started walking towards the house. "Porter is dead."

"You're kidding."

"Jessie called all hysterical saying something about a murder."

"Oh, my God," said Bert. "A real murder right here in Steam Corners."

They stepped onto the porch. "Just don't touch anything," said Calvin.

"Come on. I'm not that dumb."

"Bet me."

As they approached the house, the front screen door swung open, and Jessie was standing in the doorway.

"I heard you pull up, but I wanted to be sure it was you," she said. "Come in."

The two men stepped inside the door and turned their attention to the lifeless body and pools of blood on the floor in front of them.

"Good Lord!" said Bert. "I've never seen such a…"

Calvin turned to Jessie. "Who did this, Jessie? Do you have any idea?"

"Yeah, I know exactly who did it. It was that boy I hired to fix up the barn."

"Do you know where he is now?"

"All I know is he lives out there in the bunkhouse," she said. "Where he is after all this, I have no idea."

"Do you have a key to the bunkhouse?"

Jessie reached for the windowsill, picked up a key and handed it to Calvin.

"You wait here," said Calvin. "Come on, Bert. Let's see if he's out in the bunkhouse."

They walked across the yard to the bunkhouse. Calvin quietly slipped the key into the door lock and swung the door open. Bert felt around the side of the door until he was able to snap on a light. Spencer was asleep in his bed. His head jumped from the offensive light. Bert pulled his revolver and held it at his side.

"Come on, boy," said Calvin. "Get your ass up."

Spencer peered through squinted eyes. "Who are you?" he asked.

"I'm Sheriff Hicks, now get up. I want to talk to you."

Spencer swung his legs around to the side of the bed. "What have I done?" he asked rubbing his eyes.

"Never mind that. Just get some clothes on and come with us."

As Spencer slipped on pants and a shirt, Calvin surveyed the room.

"That looks like a woman's shirt over there on the floor. Whose is it?" asked Calvin.

Spencer glanced across the room. "That be Mrs. Harlan's."

"What's it doing in here?"

"Ask Mrs. Harlan."

"I'm asking you."

"I'd rather not say."

"You ripped it off her, didn't you, boy?"

Spencer said nothing.

"Bert, grab that shirt and bring it along," said Calvin.

Spencer finished putting on his pants and shoes. He stood to slip a tee shirt over his head.

"Hold on there, boy," said Calvin tilting his head to see the streaks of dried blood on Spencer's chest. "What the hell happened to you?"

Spencer said nothing. He slipped a tee shirt over his head.

Calvin stepped in front of Spencer and pointed a finger at him. "You know, boy, if I were you, I'd start talking and telling me everything I want to hear, 'cause the way I see it, you're in a butt load of trouble."

"Could you, at least, tell me what I'm supposed to have done?"

"I'm gonna do better than that," said Calvin. "I'm gonna show you. Cuff him, Bert. I don't want no trouble from this one. He's too damn big, and I'm too damn fat."

Bert pulled Spencer's hands behind his back and snapped a pair of handcuffs on his wrists. They grabbed him by the arm and led him out the door.

"How did you and Porter get along," Calvin asked as they walked across the yard.

"Not very good," said Spencer.

Bert laughed. "Well, that's one more nail in his coffin."

"Bull shit," said Calvin. "At least, he was honest about that. Who the hell could get along with Porter?"

They stepped upon the porch and walked through the door. Jessie was on the other side of the kitchen. She recoiled in fear.

Bert was holding Spencer's arm. "Don't worry none, Jessie. We got the cuffs on him."

Calvin pulled out a chair. "Sit down over here. By the way, just for the records, what's your name?"

"Spencer Deacon," he said as he sat down.

"Mr. Deacon, I want you to just sit right here while I talk with Jessie over there. Do you understand?"

"Yes, sir," he said.

"Bert, I want you to stand over there, and if Mr. Deacon gets out of his chair, I want you to shoot him. You got that?"

Bert moved to a location directly behind Spencer. "Yes, sir," he said fidgeting with his revolver.

"Alright, Mrs. Harlan. Obviously, this is a crime scene. I want you to tell us exactly what happened before we take a bunch of pictures and clean up this mess. Now, go on and tell us from the beginning."

"Well, let's see. Spencer got home from his date with Tilly's girl a little after eleven. She's such a cute girl. I thought Spencer and her would make a great couple. I went out to the bunkhouse to ask him how it went. Well, let me tell you. I knew Spencer had a temper, but I had no idea. He was ranting and raving, carrying on about how she wouldn't give him any. He called her a black bitch and said he should have fucked her anyhow. Sorry, Sheriff, but that's what he said."

"That's okay," said Calvin.

"The next thing I know he's grabbing me trying to kiss me. I'm doing everything I can to fight him off, but he is such a strong man. All the while, he's telling me that I'm going to have to pay for it. If he couldn't have her, he was going to take it from me. Then, without warning, he pulled my shirt over my head and threw it on the floor." She pointed at Bert who was still holding it. "I see you found it. Thank God. It's a nice shirt."

"Please continue, Mrs. Harlan," said Calvin.

"Once he got a look at my chest, he really went crazy. I don't mind telling you, I was scared. Then it came to me. The only weapons I had were my fingernails. Every woman has them. Long fingernails that can shred the bark off a tree. Well, I scratched him, alright. You can see the blood seeping through his shirt. I think it scared him more than hurt him. All I know is he jumped back, and I took the opportunity to run."

"Did he follow you?" asked Calvin.

"Chased me all the way into the house. God, I was scared."

Calvin turned to Spencer. He was squirming in his chair with a disgusted look on his face.

"Then, what?" asked Calvin.

"We wrestled a bit. Of course, I didn't have a shirt on, so he spent a lot of time just feeling my breasts. Probably the only thing that saved me. Any ways, we fought until we were both tired and out of breath. Spencer spotted a butcher knife on the counter and grabbed it. He told me to take off my shorts. I stalled him as long as I could seeing as how I had nothing on under my shorts. Finally, he got within inches of me with that knife and told me to get naked. I had my shorts unbuttoned and halfway down when in the door came Porter."

"Was Porter drunk?" asked Calvin.

"Oh, he was drunk alright. He was staggering and falling down, but there was one thing about it. I really don't think Porter saw that knife in Spencer's hand. Drunk or not drunk, I don't think anybody in their right mind would attack a man holding a butcher knife."

"Was there a fight?"

"Not that you'd notice. Hell, it was over with in seconds. Porter simply lunged at Spencer, and Spencer stuck him with that knife. Must of hit something important, 'cause he hit the floor, twitched a bit, and was dead."

"What happened then?"

"We both stood there staring at poor old Porter. I guess we were both kinda in shock. Then, suddenly, he ran out the door."

"Did you see where he went?"

"Yeah, I stepped out on the porch. He first went over there to the garden hose and washed himself off. He then went over to the bunkhouse, and before he went inside, he flung that knife out there in them weeds. Probably won't find it 'til daylight."

"Did he leave the premises?"

"Hell, no. Ain't never seen nothing like it. Fella up and kills another and goes off to bed. I thought he was going to pack his shit and get out of here. If that don't beat all."

The room went quiet. Calvin rubbed his beard and walked aimlessly around the room. "Got any questions, Bert?"

Bert cleared his throat. "Yeah. I just want to know if you're all right, Jessie. I mean he didn't hurt you or anything, did he?"

"Oh, how sweet of you, Bert," she said with a smile. "I'm just fine. You know me, tougher than leather."

Calvin put both hands on his hips and stared at the dead body with the pool of dried blood. He turned and stared at Spencer. "Tell me something, Jessie. You say that Spencer stuck Porter in the stomach with a knife. Must have squirted a long ways. In fact, I see signs that it shot over there on that kitchen cabinet."

"Never seen anything like it," she said. "Shot like a geyser."

Calvin turned and pointed at Spencer. "Was that the shirt he was wearing?"

"Yep, that's the one."

"Except for the spots of blood from his wounds, I don't see a speck of blood on his shirt. That seems mighty strange to me."

The smile disappeared from her face. "That it does," she said, her mind racing to find an answer. "Now that I think about it, Spencer was off to the side when he stuck him."

"Oh, so that would explain why he was out of the line of fire," said Calvin.

"Yes, sir," she said.

"In spite of that, he must have had a great deal of blood on his hands, perhaps, even on his arms."

"That he did," she said. "That's why he rinsed off at the garden hose."

"Oh, yes, the garden hose. Bert, you got a flashlight in your truck?"

"Got one in the glove compartment."

"Keep an eye on things, and I'll be right back."

Calvin grabbed a flashlight from Bert's truck and walked over to the garden hose. He knelt down and shone the light over the damp area. There was a milky red stain over the entire area. He looked closer and found what appeared to be dried red paint chips. He placed a chip in the palm of his hand and returned to the house.

"I got another question for you, Jessie, if you don't mind," said Calvin.

"Go ahead," she said fidgeting with the frayed hem of her shorts.

"Tell me again what happened after Spencer here stabbed Porter. You say that you both stared at him for a while. How long do you suppose that was?"

"Oh, not long. Twenty or thirty seconds."

"Then what did he do?"

"He ran out of the house."

"How long was it before he rinsed himself off?"

"A couple minutes, I suppose. Why, Sheriff? What does this have to do with…"

"So, from the time he stabbed Porter and the time he rinsed off, no more than five minutes passed. Is that right?"

"Good God, you'd think I was on trial here," said Jessie.

"This is just a crime investigation. All we trying to do here is to get at the truth. We got to know what happened while the evidence is in front of us. Memories and photographs a month from now don't mean shit. What truly matters is learning all we can right now while it's fresh. Now answer the question."

"I forgot the question."

"From the time you say that Mr.Deacon here stabbed Porter until the time he rinsed off, would you say that less than five minutes passed?

"That's about right," she said with confidence that she had offered a safe answer.

Calvin turned to Bert. "Give me one of those little baggies you always carry. You know, the ones for evidence."

Bert fished in his shirt pocket until he found one. Calvin placed the small blood chip inside the bag.

"What do you got there, Sheriff?" asked Jessie.

"It's a small chip of dried blood I found out there by the garden hose. There were more just like it, but all I needed was one."

"What's that for?" she asked.

"It's evidence."

"What kind of evidence?"

"Oh, probably nothing at all," said Calvin. "I just like to pick up as many things along the way as I can. You just never know when something might become important."

Calvin pulled a kitchen chair across the room until it was across from Spencer. He sat down and scooted it until their knees were nearly touching. "Okay, Mr. Deacon, you've listened to all this, and you've been very patient. I looked at you while she was telling her story, and I got the impression from the look on your face that you didn't agree with all the facts. So, now it's your turn. Let's hear your side of what happened."

Spencer paused for a moment, then said, "I didn't do it."

"Well, I got someone here who says you did," said Calvin.

"She lied."

"Well, Mr. Deacon, unless you start talking, it's going to come down to your word against hers, and I think you know how that's gonna play out."

"I want a lawyer," said Spencer.

"You're going to need one, that's for sure," said Calvin then turned to Bert. "Call Benson in the morning. He's new and might be stupid enough." He turned back to Spencer. "Are you sure you don't want to give us your side of what happened?"

"Would you believe my story over hers?"

"Try me."

Spencer turned with a blank stare. "I'll do my talking with a lawyer."

Calvin slowly got to his feet. "Well, I guess we're pretty much done here." Then he walked over to the sink. "I have one more question for you, Mrs. Harlan. You say that Spencer grabbed a butcher knife to kill Porter. Where do you keep your knives?

Jessie pointed at a drawer by the sink. "In that drawer over there."

Calvin opened the drawer. "Wow, you have quite a collection of knives."

"Thank you."

"My question to you is how did Spencer know which drawer had the knives?"

"I don't know. Lucky guess?"

Calvin smiled. "I thought you said Spencer spotted the knife on the counter."

"Oh, yeah," said Jessie. "Well, I guess that explains it."

Calvin pulled out a notepad and scribbled in it.

"Why are you writing stuff down?" asked Jessie.

"Memory ain't what it used to be," said Calvin. "Mrs. Harlan, we're going to send some people out here to clean up this mess. You might want to stay with some friends until we're done."

"No, that's alright."

"Suit yourself," said Calvin. He turned to see her lighting up a cigarette. She was sitting in a kitchen chair with legs cross and one leg bobbing back and forth.

"Tell me something, Mrs. Harlan. I was always under the impression that you and Porter never really hit it off."

"We had our differences," she said taking a drag from her cigarette.

"Well, we're sitting right here beside his dead body, and I haven't once seen any grief out of you. Seems a bit strange."

Jessie's leg bobbed even faster. "We all know that Porter was not the perfect example of a human being. In fact, he was a real jerk.

"Porter was well known for his, shall we say, sexual prowess with the ladies. You're a pretty lady. In fact, you're an incredibly beautiful lady, and I hope you won't mind my saying a very sexy woman."

Jessie blushed at the compliment. "Well, thank you."

"I just got to thinking that any man who spent as much time around a woman like you would sooner or later be tempted. I gotta believe that a guy like Porter had to have hit on you."

Jessie laughed. "The guy was dedicated to getting in my pants."

"Did he ever succeed?"

Jessie's leg went still. "No, he never succeeded."

"Did he ever try to take you by force?"

Jessie jumped to her feet. "Sheriff, I'm tired. Can we continue this some other time?"

"Sure," said Calvin. "Are you going to bed?"

"Yeah, I think I will," she said and walked away.

Calvin watched as she disappeared down the hallway. "Now there's one crazy woman."

Bert smiled as he watched her walk away. "Yeah, but she's also one damn pretty lady."

"Forget it, Bert," said Calvin. "You couldn't handle something like that."

"I'd sure like to give it a try," said Bert still staring down the empty hallway.

"Come on," said Calvin starting for the door. "Grab your prisoner, and let's go lock him up."

Bert grabbed Spencer by the arm and led him to the door.

"What time is it, Bert?" Calvin asked as he held the door open.

Bert glanced at his watch. "A little after five."

"After we lock him up, let's go over to the diner and grab some breakfast."

"I thought you said you were gaining weight."

"A fella still has to eat, doesn't he?"

Chapter Nine

The jail in Steam Corners was divided into two sections separated by a steel door. The back half was made up of two jail cells, and the front half was the office. It had been over ten years since anybody had even set foot in the back half, and that was for Cletus Snyder who spent two nights in one of the cells for stealing chickens. Calvin used the front half as his office and stopped there nearly everyday.

It was late morning when the front door opened. Bert was leading Harrison Benson through the doorway by the arm.

"What's the meaning of this, Sheriff?" asked Harrison with an angry voice.

Calvin was bent over a pile of paperwork. He pushed back from his desk. "Morning, Counselor," said Calvin with a smile. "What brings you to our humble little office this fine morning?"

"You know why I'm here," said Harrison shaking free of Bert's grip. "Your boob deputy brought me here."

Calvin turned to Bert standing beside the desk. "Why, Bert, either he said you are a boob or you have boobs. Either way, I'm amused."

"Very funny, Sheriff. I don't appreciate being forced to come down here," said Harrison. "I should bring up charges of kidnapping."

"Well, what did you do to rile Bert? You must have done something."

"I told him I wouldn't defend your prisoner."

"And he brought you down here for that?"

"He called me an asshole," said Bert.

"Well, there you have it. Defamation of character."

Harrison glanced at Bert. "But he is an asshole."

"Granted, but that's beside the point. The point is why are you refusing to defend Mr. Deacon?"

"You want me to defend a black man from Detroit against the Harlan family and basically the town of Steam Corners? I'm trying to make friends here, so that I can earn a living. I will be black balled, if you will pardon the expression, from everything in this town. There won't be a soul who would be caught dead talking to me, and you know it."

"But what if you win?" said Calvin. "You'll be the smartest man in town."

"I don't even know the facts in the case, and I already know the outcome."

"That's right. You don't know the facts. Maybe if you were to listen to them, you might change your mind."

"I don't know the facts, and I don't want to know the facts," said Harrison, getting to his feet. "All I want to do is go home and paint my bedroom."

"You're the only lawyer in town," said Calvin. "Whom do you think the court is going to appoint as a public defender?"

Harrison started for the door. "I'll deal with that when it happens." He opened the door to leave. "And call off your dim wit deputy. If you want to talk to me in the future, you know where I live," he said and slammed the door behind him.

Calvin turned to Bert. "Poor fool."

"Who's a poor fool?" asked Bert.

"He thinks he's heard the last of this.

"I don't know," said Bert. "He sounded pretty definite about it."

"He'll crack," said Calvin. "He just hasn't met up with the big gun yet."

"And who would that be?" asked Bert with a smile.

"I need you to do me a favor, and it's really important," said Calvin. "I want you to somehow get the word to Tilly's girl…whatever her name is that Benson won't defend our prisoner."

"Skeeter."

"What?"

"Skeeter is the name of Tilly's daughter."

"Whatever. Now it's important that whoever you get to tell her knows that she can't say that you put her up to it."

"Why don't we just tell Tilly ourselves?" asked Bert.

"You really are a dim wit, aren't you? The girl likes Deacon in there. In fact, they just went on a date together. She will passionately make a plea to her mother, and if Tilly takes up the cause, there's no way Benson will survive. Tilly will kick his ass."

"My daughter knows Skeeter."

"Who?"

Tilly's daughter. Her name is Skeeter."

"Wonder how she got a name like that?" asked Calvin.

"Story has it that they named her for the first word she ever spoke."

"Damn," said Calvin. "Good thing she didn't say something about taking a shit."

Bert stared blankly, then smiled. "I get it. That's a good one, Cal."

Calvin got to his feet. "Let's head on out to the Harlan farm. I hear Frank is back, and we need to find that butcher knife."

It was a short drive to the Harlan farm. Calvin parked near the bunkhouse, and they both got out of the car. Within minutes of stomping in the weeds, Calvin yelled out, "Here it is, Bert. I found it." He picked up by the corner of the blade with two fingers and a handkerchief.

"Still has blood on it," said Bert.

"Someone did a poor job of rinsing it off," said Calvin. "Hope they did the same with the fingerprints." He turned to Bert. "Give me another baggie, and make it a big one."

Bert dug in his back pocket and pulled out a larger sized bag. They dropped the knife in and sealed the bag.

Just then, Calvin heard a door slam. He turned and saw a large man stepping off the porch and coming their way. Calvin handed the knife to Bert. "Quick. Take this to the car and hide it on the floor."

Bert stood motionlessly holding the knife. "Why?"

"That's Frank coming," said Calvin pointing at the knife. "The butcher knife...get it out of here."

Bert finally came to life. "Oh, yeah. The knife." He cupped it with his hand and held it next to his stomach then marched off to the car.

"Morning, Cal," said Frank with a blank face.

"Morning, Frank. Sorry about your boy."

Frank's expression didn't change. "I suppose that was the murder weapon you found out there."

"Yes, it was, Frank. We tried our best to keep it from you."

"That's okay. I suppose you got that boy locked up."

"We sure do."

Frank watched as Bert opened the car and dropped the knife inside.

"How are you doing, Frank?"

Frank either ignored the question or didn't hear it. "You best get his stuff out of that bunkhouse."

"I was going to talk to you about that," said Calvin. I need a key to lock up his belongings."

"I'm going to burn down the bunkhouse."

Calvin paused. He stared at Frank as if he had antlers. "Well, I guess I'll send someone out later today."

"I want to talk to him, Sheriff," said Frank.

"To whom?"

"Mr. Deacon. I want to talk to Mr. Deacon."

"Oh, I don't know. That's just not done. Most people don't..."

"Set it up for me. Will ya?"

"Yeah. Sure."

Bert returned and sensed the tension. He said nothing.

"Are we through here?" asked Frank.

"For now," said Calvin.

Without so much as another word, Frank turned and walked away.

"What was that all about?"

"Frank wants to see Deacon."

"Is that legal?" asked Bert.

"All I know is we're going to have to be real careful when it happens. The look on Frank's face turned my blood cold."

"Do you think he'd kill him if he had the chance?"

"He looked as if he'd do it with or without the chance," said Calvin.

They turned and started for the car.

"Maybe that would be the best thing," said Bert.

"Maybe what would be the best thing?"

"Let Frank have the satisfaction of doing it," said Bert. "After all, the boy is guilty. What makes the difference how he gets it?"

"In the first place, he ain't guilty until proven so in a court of law," said Calvin. "And in the second place, we'd just have to lock up Frank."

"That don't seem fair," said Bert.

"I get fatter all the time, and you don't. What's fair about that?"

"It's in the genes, Calvin. You don't take care of your genes."

"Get in the car, Bert.

***

Nightfall brought a cool breeze that drifted through open windows bringing peace and a sense of relief to the little town of Steam Corners. Tilly was in the kitchen putting away the last of the dishes from dinner when Skeeter entered the room. There was a distressed look on her face.

"Where's Mr. Benson?" asked Skeeter.

"I don't know, child. He said something about going out on the porch. He's probably sittin' on the porch soakin' up some of that cool night air. Why?"

"I got something to ask you, and I didn't want him to hear."

Tilly wiped her hands on a towel and sat down at the table. "What is it, child? It looks pretty serious."

"I found out today that Mr. Benson won't defend Spencer."

"My, I wonder why," said Tilly as if she were thinking aloud. Don't make sense. Sounds like a great opportunity for a young lawyer."

"Could it be because he's black?"

"What do you mean, child?"

"Maybe he don't like black folks and wants to see Spencer hang or whatever they do."

"Oh, good Lord, no," said Tilly with a smile of confidence. "That man is way above that kind of thinking. Ain't nobody know him better than me. Been with him most all of his life. No. There has to be another reason."

"Talk him into it, mama," said Skeeter taking her mother's hand.

"What?"

"Talk him into defending Spencer. He's Spencer's only chance."

"I can't do that. I might wash his socks and cook him his meals, but I don't ever mess with Mr. Benson's business."

Skeeter cupped her mother's hand with both of hers. "I never asked you for anything like this in my life. All I'm asking is that you try. That's all. I got a good feeling about Spencer Deacon. I'm not saying I love the man. I just met him. All I'm saying is I know in my heart he didn't do it. There's no way that man killed Mr. Harlan."

Tilly lightly gripped her daughter's hand. "You wait here, and I'll go see what I can do. No promises now. He's a stubborn man, but I'll give it a try."

"Thanks," she said with a smile.

Tilly got to her feet and started across the room. As she stepped outside on the porch, she felt a cool breeze. Harrison was reading the paper by the light from the living room window.

Tilly took a deep breath. "Feels good out here."

"Can't figure why it cooled off like that," said Harrison. "Must be a storm coming."

"Can't remember the last time we had a good old fashioned summer storm," said Tilly.

"I would settle for the rain," said Harrison.

"Mind if I sit for a spell?"

"Have a seat."

Tilly sat down next to him on the swing.

"What's on your mind?" Harrison asked.

"Why do you ask that? Maybe I came out here to cool off."

"I've known you too long."

"Well, I've got something to discuss with you, and I don't really know how to do it."

"Since when have you ever had a shy bone in your body?"

"You know me, Mr. Benson. I might tell you to pick your socks off the floor, but I don't meddle in your business."

Harrison smiled. "You want to know why I don't want to represent Mr. Deacon, don't you?"

"Like I said before, it's none of my business, but it just seems to me that would be a great opportunity for a young man like yourself. He's obviously going to be charged with murder. You get him off, and you become the hero of the year."

Harrison folded his paper and dropped it to the floor. "Tilly, you know if it was right for me, I'd do it in a heartbeat if for no other reason than for Skeeter. But taking this case would be suicide. Think about it. You're asking me to defend a black man from the city of Detroit against the town of Steam Corners. Not only would I alienate myself whether I won or not, I would never get anybody to hire me again."

Tilly paused as she thought about what he had said. "So what you're saying is you don't want to take the case because you might lose some business? How much business are you doing now?"

"That's not the point."

"Seems to me you got nothing to lose."

"That might be so, but…"

"I think you need to shake things up a bit. You need to show these people around here just what you're made of."

Harrison said nothing.

"Besides, I thought you lawyer people were supposed to defend us folk right or wrong. Weren't you fellers supposed to sign some kind of oath?"

"That's doctors," said Harrison. "Doctors sign an oath."

"Well, aren't you supposed to serve and protect?"

"That's the police."

"Land's sakes," she said. "I know you people are supposed to do something. I may not know much, but I do know one thing. If you're even half the man I think you are, you'll make sure that boy gets a fair trial. After all, Mr. Benson, the cards are stacked against him, and you know it."

Harrison paused, then slowly shook his head. "I don't believe what you're doing to me."

Tilly smiled. "Then, you will defend him?"

"I didn't say that," he said. "I will, however, talk to him. That's all I can promise."

"Thank you, Mr. Benson. Thank you so much. God looks after good people like you."

"I hope so, because I'm going to need all the help I can get."

Tilly got to her feet. "Can I get you anything?"

"Don't suck up to me, Tilly," he said. "It's unbecoming of you."

"It's only this one time," she said with a sneer.

"Oh, well, in that case, I'll take a cup of coffee."

"Sorry, but you had your chance and blew it," she said and walked away.

The next morning brought the promise of another hot day. Harrison stopped by the diner for breakfast and took a seat at a long row of tables filled with men. He sat next to his friend, Clyde Butts, and as he did, the conversation hushed at the table and all eyes turned to him.

"Morning, Butts," said Harrison.

"I wish you wouldn't call me that," he said.

"What do you want me to call you?"

"How 'bout Clyde? That's my name."

"I thought your name was Butts."

"Well, it's Mr. Butts to you."

Harrison glanced up and down the table. "What's going on? Everybody looks so mysterious."

"They're all wondering if you're going to represent that kid."

A waitress sped by dropping off a cup of coffee. "How do you want 'em?" she asked over her shoulder as she walked away.

"Scrambled," said Harrison, watching her nearly run away. "Nice looking lady."

"Great ass," said Clyde, staring as well.

"So what if I do represent the kid?"

"I'd watch my back if I were you."

"You can't be serious."

"These people want him dead."

"I don't believe it," said Harrison.

"Don't forget, you're dealing with a bunch of rednecks here. They really don't want to wait until the trial is over."

"What are you saying?"

"I'm saying they want him dead right now, if you catch what I mean."

"Vigilante style?"

Clyde leaned over and whispered, "I heard once that years ago, there was a black man waiting trial for raping a white girl, and the good old boys took justice into their own hands."

"What did they do?"

Clyde leaned even closer. "You ain't going to believe it, but they took that boy out in the woods and nailed his dick to a log. They then left a knife beside him and set the log on fire."

"Good Lord."

"Needless to say, that boy bled to death after cutting his own pecker off."

"Where do you hear this stuff?"

Clyde nodded his head at the others.

The waitress ran by dropping a plate of food in front of Harrison. He stared at the eggs, bacon, and toast.

"What if I wanted sausage instead?" he asked to no one in particular.

Clyde laughed. "Do you remember Lum Harper from high school days? If you remember right, Lum wasn't the brightest bulb in the box. The way he figures it, whatever he has on the grill at the time you order is what you get. He has said more than once that it all comes from the same hog.

Harrison picked up a strip of bacon and took a bite. "So what you're saying is I shouldn't take this case."

"Can't imagine anybody hiring you if you do, and, unless I miss my guess, you ain't gonna get rich on that kid."

Harrison took a quick glance down the table. "Is there nobody who believes that everyone is entitled to a fair trial by a jury even if he is a black kid from Detroit?"

"Nobody from these parts," said Clyde with a fiendish smile. "Besides, he's pretty much already been tried and convicted by his peers. The only thing left now is the execution."

Harrison stopped eating and turned to Clyde. "They wouldn't really do anything like that, would they?"

Clyde said nothing. He smiled and continued to eat his breakfast.

"It's hard to believe in this day and age we would be having this conversation," said Harrison.

"So, tell me," said Clyde, leaning back in his chair and wiping his mouth with his shirtsleeve. "Are you going to represent him?"

"I don't know," said Harrison staring blankly at his plate. "I haven't even talked with him yet."

"Well, what's your gut reaction?"

"Why? What makes the difference?" Harrison asked. He turned towards Clyde and was stunned by his strange smile. Clyde simply nodded at the other men sitting at the table who had all but frozen waiting for an answer from Harrison.

"I don't get it," said Harrison. "Do they want me to take the case or not?"

"Some do, and some don't."

"What's that supposed to mean?"

"The ones who want you to take the case, think you'll lose, and the ones who don't want you to take the case are hoping nobody will defend him."

Harrison scanned the table of men and studied the quiet faces. A look of determination swept across Harrison's face. He jumped to his feet. "Guess I'll go talk to the young man. Looks as if he could use all the help he can get."

It was late morning when Harrison opened the front door to the jail. Calvin was asleep with his chair leaning against the wall. Harrison slammed the door behind him, and the noise startled Calvin.

"Jesus, son of Mary," muttered Calvin leaning forward to return the chair to its upright position.

"Sheriff, I need to talk to your prisoner," said Harrison.

Calvin scrambled to his feet. "I knew you'd be coming around. You lawyer fellers can't resist the challenge."

"Challenge? This is a surefire case of suicide for me. What chance does this boy have?"

"The way I see it is he has no chance at all if you don't represent him," said Calvin. "Besides, it's about time you got your feet wet."

Calvin led Harrison to the backroom and unlocked the cell door. "You know I'm supposed to pat you down right now, but I never was crazy about doing that to a man."

"I promise I'm not smuggling in any weapons or hacksaws."

"Good enough for me," said Calvin and swung the door open. "I'm leaving the door unlocked while you're in there. Just pull it shut when you leave."

Spencer, who had been sitting on the edge of his bed, sprung to his feet.

Harrison stuck out his hand. "The name's Harrison Benson."

Spencer took his hand. "I feel like I already know you."

"How's that?"

"Skeeter talks about you all the time."

Harrison took a quick look at the room. It had a bed, a rocking chair and the walls had two landscape paintings and a calendar. "Pretty cozy for a jail cell," he said taking a seat in the rocking chair.

"Actually, this is much better than what I had when I lived in Detroit."

Harrison opened a small notebook and clicked his ballpoint to life. "So, tell me, Mr. Deacon, what was that like?"

"Call me Spencer."

"If that's what you want."

"What was what like?"

"Living in Detroit. What was that like?"

Spencer squirmed and glanced around the floor. "I guess the best word to describe it is depressing. If you're born in trash, you begin to think and act like trash. I knew at an early age that I wanted more for my life."

"What about your parents? What kind of influence did they have?"

"There are no parents where I come from," said Spencer. "Either your father ran away when he heard your mother was pregnant, or your mother ain't quite sure which one was the daddy. Either way, you got a lot of mothers trying to raise a bunch of kids, and it don't always work out."

"Where does she get the money?"

"Most mothers try to do it on welfare, and, if you know anything about the welfare system, you know that it ain't enough to live on. Like my mother, some go to work. Of course, that leaves her kids at home with nobody to watch them. That's a bad situation, but what is she to do?"

Harrison paused as he scribbled notes. "Where are the fathers while this is going on?"

"Who knows? Out making babies with other women."

Harrison stopped writing. He tilted his head and looked at Spencer over his glasses. "Sounds depressing."

"I believe that's the word I used earlier."

"So, what about you? Why didn't you fall into the same rut?"

"I was digging through a trashcan and found an old copy of a magazine called, *Country Living*. Why I picked it up, I'll never know, and how it got there is as big a mystery. It ain't exactly the kind of reading material that you find in the ghetto. Anyways, I started reading about farms and small town life. It even had pictures. At the time, I remember thinking that kind of life would never be meant for someone like me. That was for white people only. A black boy like me would never be allowed in a place like that. No, siree."

"But you made it," said Harrison with a slight grin. "You got out of the city, and here you are in a small town."

Spencer gave a sarcastic laugh and glanced around the room. "Yeah, I made it alright. I'm right where every black man belongs. The only difference is I'm in a small town jail instead of one in the city."

There was an awkward silence.

"So tell me, Spencer," said Harrison. "What happened that night?"

"What makes the difference? Nobody is going to believe me."

Harrison stuck the pencil between the pages and closed his notebook. "Look, Spencer. I haven't agreed to defend you. At this point, I'm simply gathering facts to see if we have a case. If you want me as your defense attorney, you must tell me everything no matter how much you might think it will be harmful to you. I must know everything. I can't run the risk of being blind-sighted in court."

Spencer slowly shook his head. "Just looks to me that it's gonna be my word against Mrs. Harlan's."

"It will if you don't let me do my job, but you have to tell me everything."

Spencer searched Harrison's face for a sign of sincerity. "Ain't much to tell."

Harrison reopened his notebook and took the pencil. "Then this won't take long."

"Well, sir," said Spencer staring blankly at the floor. "That night I had a date with Skeeter. I had her home by eleven 'cause Miss Tilly told me to, and I sure don't want to upset that woman. When I got home I could see Mrs. Harlan sitting on the edge of the porch. I knew she'd been drinking since she went and threw a beer bottle and it clinked when it hit the others. Next thing I knew, she was in the bunkhouse wanting me to have sex with her. When I refused, she got real mad and started hitting me. She even scratched up my chest. She finally left, and the next thing I knew, Sheriff Hicks is standing over my bed accusing me of killing Porter. I swear to God I didn't even see that man that evening, alive that is."

"Are you saying you saw Porter after he was dead?" asked Harrison.

"Yes, sir," said Spencer. "Sheriff Hicks put handcuffs on me and led me up to the house."

"Why did he do that?"

"I guess just to question me and Mrs. Harlan."

"I hope you didn't incriminate yourself by something you said."

"I ain't sure what that means."

"Did you tell him anything he could use against you in a court of law?"

"I don't think so, unless telling the truth is a bad thing, 'cause that's what I did. I told him the truth."

Harrison scribbled some notes. "Tell me something, Spencer. How did Mrs. Harlan react when you entered the kitchen?"

"What d'ya mean?"

"Did she run or scream? After all, you had supposedly just tried to rape her."

"No, nothing like that."

"Was she crying? Did she show any sorrow at all from the shock of seeing her stepson killed?"

"No, sir," said Spencer. There we was sitting in that kitchen with a dead man on the floor. She never flinched. Just like any other day for her."

"You said earlier," said Harrison scanning his notes, "That Mrs. Harlan tried to get you to have sex with her. Is that correct?"

"Yes."

"Had she ever done that before?"

"Many times."

"Did you ever have sex with her?"

"No, sir."

"Why is that? She's an attractive woman. You must have thought about it."

"Oh, I thought about it," said Spencer. "I won't deny that. She's one pretty lady, that's for sure."

"She must have been fairly persistent. Why didn't you take her up on it?"

"Oh, there be many reasons, Mr. Benson. "For one thing, you know as well as I do, if I ever did such a thing and folks found out about it... Besides, such a thing is a sin."

Harrison wrote more notes in his book. "So, are you telling me that you're religious?"

"I believe in God, if that's what you mean."

"Do you go to church?"

"I did back home. Ain't found a church around here for black folks."

"Let me see if I got this straight," said Harrison. "Due to your religious background and moral upbringing, you consider adultery a sin. Is that right?"

"Yes, sir."

"Do you have any idea what type of woman Jessie is?"

"No, sir."

"Well, you must have some kind of an opinion."

"It's not for me to judge others," said Spencer. "I leave that to God."

Harrison finished writing in his notebook. "Do you have anything else to say?"

"I was just wondering if you are going to help me."

Harrison closed his notebook and got to his feet. "I know I should have my head examined, but, yes, I'm going to take your case.

Spencer jumped up and looked Harrison in the eyes. "I just wanted you to know that I didn't kill Porter Harlan. I just hope you believe me."

"It's not important whether or not I believe you. I only have to provide the best defense I can."

"But it is important," said Spencer. "It's important that you believe me."

Harrison stared into Spencer's eyes for a few moments thinking about what to say. "Don't worry about a thing, Mr. Deacon. I believe you and will do everything in my power to get you free."

"Thank you, Mr. Benson," said Spencer.

Harrison walked out of the jail cell and slammed the steel door behind him. Calvin was leaning over paperwork when Harrison stepped into his office.

"Let me guess, Counselor," said Calvin. "You're going to take his case."

"I must be out of my head," said Harrison.

Calvin leaned back in his chair. "I knew you couldn't resist."

Harrison sat in a wooden chair that creaked as if it were coming apart. "So, tell me, Sheriff, you were there to investigate the murder. What's your opinion? Did he do it?"

"If my opinion ever counted for anything, I would say he didn't do it."

"Whoa. I wasn't expecting that. Why do you think he is innocent?"

"Just too many little things...things that don't add up. Why would this Deacon kid simply go back to bed after killing another human being? I would have been long gone to another county."

"Anything else?"

"More than I got time for," said Calvin. "Why don't you stop back sometime?"

"Will do," said Harrison. "One more question, did Deacon give you any trouble?"

"What do you mean?"

"When you took him in. Did he try to run or get away from you? Did he resist arrest in any way?"

"No, not a bit," said Calvin. "If the truth be known, he's too nice of a kid for that."

Harrison picked up his briefcase and started for the door. "You know you're going to be my star witness."

Calvin laughed. "The way I got it figured, I'll probably be your only witness."

It was early evening when Jessie reported for work. As soon as she stepped inside the bar, Earl motioned for her to come over to his table. "Have a seat," he said scooting his chair closer to hers. "Are you okay?"

"Oh, I'm fine," she said.

"Rumor has it that black boy is in jail."

"As usual, your sources are accurate," she said lighting a cigarette.

"Is it true he killed Porter?"

"Stuck him with a knife," she said with a shudder. "God, it was awful."

"What happened anyhow?"

"Ever since he moved in, Spencer has been trying to get me in bed."

"Why didn't you tell me?"

"I just figured he would soon get the hint," she said. "I mean, after all, I never gave him any idea that he even had a chance."

"That son-of-a-bitch," muttered Earl. "I should have run his ass out of town the first day he showed up."

"Last night he came home after a date. He was acting kinda strange. I'm not sure if he was drunk or what. Said something about not getting any, and the next thing I know he's all over me."

"Did he rape you?"

"No. He never got that far. I was able to fight him off for a while. The next thing I knew Porter was walking though the front door. Spencer instinctively picked up a butcher knife and stabbed Porter as he lunged at him.

Earl began to fume. "Did he die right away or did he suffer?"

"He twitched for a few moments then was still."

"I was never a big fan of Porter, but he didn't deserve that," said Earl.

Jessie looked away as if she were remembering the scene. "I never seen so much blood."

Earl leaned forward and touched her arm. "To be honest, I always thought you would be the one to take Porter out."

"Why would you say that?" she asked.

"I don't know," said Earl easing back in his chair. "Guess I kinda figured you two didn't get along so good."

"Maybe so, but he was my stepson."

Earl became silent. His stare turned to the top of his table. "It ain't right for some nigger comin' here to town and killin' one of our own. It just ain't right."

Jessie smiled. "You sound as if you're about to take matters into your own hands."

"Now don't you never mind about that," he said clenching his fists. "The less you know the better off you'll be."

"Well, at least, we have one real man in this town."

"I thought I heard that Frank was back in town already," said Earl. "Is he okay with you working here?"

"He thinks I'm working at the diner."

"Don't you think you should tell him?"

Jessie looked away with a disgusted look on her face. "I suppose."

"You don't want him to find out from someone else."

"He ain't gonna like it."

"The worst part of it is he just lost his son," said Earl. "He don't need more bad news."

Just then, the front door opened, and four men walked in. They scanned the bar until their eyes fell on Earl.

"Go on get out of here," said Earl looking at Jessie. "I've got business with these men."

Jessie got to her feet with a disgruntled look on her face. She started to protest when she finally realized what kind of business Earl meant.

"Bring some beer over here for the boys, will ya?" asked Earl.

"Sure will," she said and started for the bar.

Earl got to his feet as the four men approached his table. "Sit down boys. I got beer on the way."

As the men took seats around the table, Jessie set a tray of assorted kinds of beer in the middle of the table.

"Gentlemen, I suppose you're all wondering why I called a meeting on such short notice," said Earl scanning the table and making eye contact with each man. "We got a problem."

"It's that nigger locked up in Calvin's jail, isn't it?" asked Charlie Higgins.

"We got to do something about him," said Earl. "He's got to pay for what he did."

"Is it true?" asked Ned Ballows. "Did he really kill Porter Harlan?"

"Stuck him with a butcher knife," said Earl. "Then walked off to the bunkhouse and went to sleep. How's that for a set of balls?"

The table went silent as each man tried to imagine the heinous act.

"Why did he do it?" asked Charlie.

"Porter walked in on him trying to rape Jessie, and he tried to stop him"

Charlie sat straight in his chair. "That boy tried to rape Jessie? Shit, man, he should die for that alone."

Ned leaned forward and lowered his voice to a whisper. "If we allow some black boy to come down here from Detroit and try to rape one of our women then kill one of our honest, law-abiding citizens, there's no tellin' what would happen."

"I'm telling you we got to nip this thing in the bud right here and now," said Charlie.

Earl gulped his beer. "That's why I called you boys here tonight. We got to work out a plan."

"A plan to do what?" asked Ned with a grin.

Earl dismissed the question with a wave of his hand. "We all know what we're here for."

"What about Calvin?" said Charlie. "He's not going to let us just walk in that jail and take him."

"We need a distraction," said Earl. "And it has to be somewhere far from town."

"Y'all know where I live," said Ned. "I'm damn near in the next county."

"Suppose you could get Calvin out to your place?"

"Better make it good. Calvin ain't no dummy. My guess he's figuring on something like this."

"Don't worry. I'll get him out there one way or the other."

"What about Bert?" asked Charlie.

"No doubt Calvin will leave Bert behind to keep an eye on things," said Earl. "We'll have to overtake him then lock him up in one of the cells."

"What are we going to do to him, Earl?" asked Ned.

"What d'ya mean?"

"You know..."

There was a long pause. "I say we hang him," said Earl. "Ain't nothing like a good hanging to send a message to the others."

"A good horse-whippin' would make him suffer longer," said Charlie.

"Take too long," said Earl. "I figure we got just so much time before one of our do-good citizens calls Cal. Then we got what maybe fifteen minutes for him to get back here?"

"Maybe sooner if he punches it," said Ned.

Earl finished his beer and slid the empty bottle to the middle of the table. "Alright, boys, are we all in agreement?"

They all looked at each other and cautiously nodded their heads.

"Alright then, tomorrow night nine o'clock. Everybody in full garb. Now, get out of here," said Earl.

Chapter Ten

The next morning ushered in another hot, sultry day. Frank poured himself a cup of coffee and took a seat at the kitchen table. He slowly scanned the room until his eyes fell on a splattering of red on the front of a kitchen cabinet. At first, he didn't recognize the strange looking substance, then it hit him. It was dried blood. It was the same blood that had shot from a mortal wound sustained by his only son.

It had been a nightmare since he first learned of Porter's death, a nightmare that just wouldn't end. Porter was never a model child. Lord knows he required constant supervision and discipline, but he didn't deserve this. Nobody should have to die like this.

Frank lit a cigarette and sipped his coffee. His eyes drifted to the void outside the window, his mind to a time when Porter merrily chased at his father's heels. It was the springtime of the year, and ten year old Porter had just opened his birthday present, a Red Ryder BB gun. It was cocked and loaded and he was prowling the wilds of his backyard. At first, he searched the bushes for any bears or other ferocious wildlife. Then, he turned his attention to the treetops searching for any unsuspecting robin or blue jay that had dared to land in his backyard and ultimately in his cross hairs.

Then, it happened. From out of nowhere, a mother robin appeared. Sitting proudly on a branch near the top of the tree, it stared defiantly at the young boy and his weapon. He raised his gun and took aim. He held his breath and slowly squeezed the trigger. The gun jolted and made a dull report. Seconds later, the lifeless body of a young female robin fell from its high perch crashing against branch after branch until it finally hit the ground.

Porter walked over to his prey and knelt down beside it. With the butt of his gun, he cautiously poked at it but got no response. He poked it again. Still nothing. The young boy sat down on the grass and began to cry.

Frank smiled as he remembered his son and the grief he felt for the fallen bird. It had cost the life of a robin but had taught a young boy a valuable lesson. Frank's eyes strayed back to the blood-splattered cabinet. Tears welled in his eyes and spilled down his cheeks. He sobbed aloud covering his face with his hands.

Just then, Jessie stepped into the kitchen. She froze at the sight of this strong man sobbing uncontrollably. She pulled up a chair and put her arm around his shoulders.

"Sorry," he said wiping the tears from his eyes. "I guess it finally hit me, losing my son and all."

"That's all right, Frank," she said. "You have every right."

"Don't know why it took so long to hit me."

"You've been busy, so busy with details. Your heart just hadn't caught up with your brain."

"I suppose you're right," he said getting to his feet. He refilled his coffee cup and returned to his seat. "I know he could be a handful at times, but he was my son."

"We're all going to miss him," said Jessie taking away her hand.

Frank paused. "Are we?" he asked without turning around.

"What do you mean by that?" she asked.

"Are you going to miss him?" he asked turning to face her.

"Sure, I'm going to miss him. He was my stepson. Why would you ask such a question?"

"For one thing I haven't seen one tear from you."

"I've had my private moments."

"Come on, Jessie," he said. "Tell the truth. You hated his guts, and you're glad he's dead."

"I didn't say that. I didn't even think that."

"All I want to know is why. Why did you hate him so much?"

"Alright, Frank. Maybe this isn't the best time for this, but you're asking the question, and I guess you deserve the answer. You have no idea what he was like when you weren't around. I don't think a day went by that he didn't hit on me. He was disgusting, Frank, absolutely disgusting. Everyday I was afraid of being raped."

"You can't rape the willing," he muttered.

"What did you say?"

"You heard me. Was he trying to get you in bed, or was it the other way around?"

Jessie's eyebrows furrowed. "How could you say such a thing?"

"Come on, Jessie, we all know what kind of woman you are."

"And just what kind of woman am I?"

"I shouldn't have to tell you that. You know how you are when it comes to sex."

"Oh, now I see where this is going. Because I like sex, I'm the evil one. Did you ever think I might be normal, and you are the strange one? After all, Frank, most couples have sex more than once a year, and the only reason we have it that much is because of me. If I didn't start something, we wouldn't do it at all."

Frank turned away. "That's enough, Jessie."

"No, I'm not finished," she said nearly shouting. "You might think of me as a tramp and a whore, but I never gave your son any encouragement or an idea that I might be interested. Good Lord, he was my stepson. You don't have sex with a stepson."

Frank still had his back to her. "I'm going to go meet Mr. Deacon."

"Why are you going to do that?"

"I want to hear his side of all this."

Jessie paused. A look of panic spread across her face. "How could you possibly trust what he would tell you. After all, he is a nigger, and all niggers lie, they cheat and they steal."

Frank looked over his shoulder. "You were the one who hired this man. Why would you hire someone you consider to be a liar and thief?"

"Because I thought he was different. He seemed like such a nice boy, but, oh, was I ever wrong about that."

"Be as it may, I need to talk to him."

"Why?" she asked. "If you know he's a liar, how could you possibly believe anything he might say?"

Frank got to his feet and started across the room. "When I look him in the eyes, I'll know the truth." He opened the door and walked out of the house.

Calvin was sitting at his desk when Frank walked in. He snubbed out his cigar and leaned back in his chair. "Morning, Frank."

"Morning, Cal," he said.

"Hot enough for ya?"

"Not here for small talk, Calvin," he said.

"Kinda figured you'd be comin' around."

"Can I talk to your prisoner?"

"Sit down, Frank."

"I'm fine standing."

"Frank, you and I have been friends for a long time. You know as well as I do that if folks found out I let you in there, I'd lose my job."

"You gonna let me in there or not?"

"Just hold on there, Frank, you gotta make me a promise that you won't tell a soul."

"Can't make any promises like that."

"Holy Moses, you ain't making it any easier on me."

"Sorry about that."

"Carrying any weapons?"

"Huh?"

"Do you have a gun on you?"

"You know me better than that, Cal."

"I had to ask," said Calvin. He pointed at a door at the rear of the room. "It's unlocked, and there's a chair right outside his cell. You got ten minutes."

Frank flashed him a cold stare.

"Alright, you got as long as you need," said Calvin.

Frank slowly opened the steel door and pushed it open. His eyes fell on a young black man dressed in jeans and a tee shirt and sitting on the edge of his bed.

"Mr. Deacon?" said Frank.

"Call me Spencer."

"I'm Frank Harlan."

Spencer jumped to his feet. "Yes, sir."

"Sit down, Mr. Deacon."

Spencer slowly eased himself back down. "If you don't mind my saying so, I didn't expect to see you here."

Frank sat on the wooden chair next to the cell. "They tell me you're from Detroit."

"Yes, sir."

"What are you doing down here?"

"I don't know how familiar you are with Detroit, but it or any other city is the kind of place I want to live."

"Why not?"

"People just don't care about one another like they do here in a small town."

"So, you would characterize yourself as a person who cares about others. Is that right?"

"Yes, sir," said Spencer. "Pardon me, Mr. Harlan, but would you mind telling me why you're asking all these questions?"

"Mr. Deacon, there are people who are convinced that you killed my son. I just want to find out for myself."

Spencer shifted his weight on the bed. "Fair enough, Mr. Harlan."

"Do you go to church?" asked Frank.

"I did back in Detroit."

"Why don't you go to church around here?"

"Haven't found a church for my people."

"What if you came to my church?"

"I don't think that would be a good idea," said Spencer with an embarrassed look.

Frank paused. "They tell me you had a date that night with Tilly's daughter. Is that right?"

"Yes, sir."

"How did that go?"

"Real fine, sir. She's a real nice girl."

"What did you do on your date?"

"Oh, we must have talked the whole night away," said Spencer with a smile. "I went and took her out to the diner, but what we did is talk about different things."

"What kind of things?"

"Oh, let me see. We talked a great deal about life in a small town and life in the city. Talked about God, religion and things. I don't know, just stuff. She sure is easy to talk to and real pretty to look at."

"Were you planning on seeing her again?"

"Well, yes, I was right up until this here happened."

"So, it's safe to say that you were in a pretty good mood after that date."

"Oh, yes, sir. I was on cloud nine, as they say."

Frank scooted his chair closer and leaned forward. "Okay, Mr. Deacon, I want you to tell me what happened that night after you got home from your date."

Spencer stiffened. "I don't know, sir, whether I should or not."

"Why is that?"

"You ain't gonna like what I got to say."

"Tell me anyhow."

"It's about your wife."

"I already figured that much. It's okay. Just tell me the truth."

"Well, sir, I don't mean to sound disrespectful, but your wife has more or less been interested in me ever since she hired me. I could be wrong, but that's the impression I got." Spencer paused and searched Frank for a reaction.

"Go ahead," he said.

"Well, sir, she'd a been drinking that night. That was plain to see. I ain't never seen her that way, so I went straight for the bunkhouse to go to bed. Next thing I know, she's a walking into the bunkhouse and wanting me to go to bed with her. Hell, she even took off her top right there in front of me. I up and turned her down, and I don't think she liked that too much. Next thing I know she's beating on me and scratching my chest and arms. I never seen a woman so mad. Once I got her out of there, I watched as she staggered up to the house. Once I saw her go inside, I went to bed."

"What happened then?" asked Frank.

"Next thing I know there's the sheriff standing over me and I'm accused of murder."

"Did you kill my son?"

"Sir?"

Frank leaned even closer. "Did you kill my son?"

"No, sir, I didn't," said Spencer. "I'll be honest, Mr. Harlan, I didn't care much for your son, but I'd never kill him."

"Well, if you didn't kill him, who did?"

Spencer paused. He had a look of apprehension. "Can't say for a fact."

"You have your suspicions, don't you?"

"Yes, sir."

"Well then, who killed my son?"

"It just wouldn't be right for me to accuse somebody without any facts."

"Seems to me that's what they're doing to you," said Frank.

"Yes, sir, but that don't make it right for me to do the same."

Frank got to his feet. "Thank you for your time, Mr. Deacon," he said starting for the door. "Sorry to have bothered you."

"Mr. Harlan," said Spencer.

Frank had already opened the door. He turned back to Spencer. "Yes."

"What's going to happen to me?"

"It appears you're going to go to trial."

"What if they find me guilty?"

"I wouldn't worry about that right now."

"I learned a lesson from this. That's for sure.

"And what's that?"

"I should have stayed in Detroit."

It was early afternoon when the front door of the jail opened. Calvin looked up from his desk to see Jessie closing the door behind her. His mouth dropped open. "Good Lord, what are you doing here?"

"Nice to see you too, Calvin," she said with a hint of sarcasm.

"I gotta tell ya, you're the last person I expected to see in here."

"I came here to see Spencer."

"Well, I suppose it wouldn't hurt none," he said then pointed at the door. "He's right through there. By the way, you didn't bring a hacksaw with you, did you?"

Jessie said nothing. She turned and shot Calvin a look of disdain. She opened the door and stepped inside. Spencer was lying on the bed. When he saw her enter the room, he jumped up and sat on the edge of the bed.

"Hi, Spencer," she said with an air of tension in her voice. "How are you?"

Spencer quickly rubbed his head with both hands. "I'm fine. Thank you for asking."

"Is Calvin treating you okay?" she asked taking a seat on the only chair in the room.

"Oh, yes, ma'am. That he is."

"I hear the food ain't too bad in here."

"Why are you doing this to me?"

"Huh?"

"Why did you accuse me of killing Porter? You know I didn't do it. Why are you doing this to me?"

"How do I know you didn't?" she said. "I wasn't in the kitchen when he was killed. It could have been you."

"You did it, didn't you, Mrs. Harlan?"

"Are you accusing me of killing my own stepson?" she said with an angry voice. "How dare you."

"I'm not accusing you of anything since I didn't actually see you do it," he said. "I simply asked you if you did it."

"Of course, I didn't do it. Why would you ask?"

"It would seem to me that since there were only three of us out there at the time and since one of them is dead and I know I didn't do it, that logically leaves you."

"Somebody like a tramp could have happened along and done it," she said.

"Come on, Mrs. Harlan," said Spencer with a lowered voice. "It's just you and me here. I think I deserve to know why you did it."

Jessie paused, then with a nearly muted voice said, "You wouldn't understand."

"Try me."

"He was an animal, an absolute animal. All he ever thought about was himself," she said.

"He tried to rape you that night, didn't he?"

"He tried to rape me everyday of my life, and that night was no different."

"I've always said that everybody has their breaking point."

Jessie turned and stared blankly at the wall. "He was drunk that night, really drunk. I don't think I ever saw him that bad, and there I was with no top on. He went crazy out of his head. He'd never seen me like that, or at least I never knew of it. Sometimes I was wondered if he was looking at me when I was in the shower. There was a keyhole in the door, and sometimes I swear I could see him on the other side."

"So he came after you that night, and the knife was close by."

"God help me, but it felt good when it happened. I never thought I'd see the day when killing a man would feel that good. He didn't even see it coming. You're right. The knife was close by. I don't think he even saw me pick it up. It was over in seconds. Hell, he was so drunk I don't think he even had pain from it.

"Then why me? Why did you blame it on me?"

"You said it best. There was only the three of us out there. If it wasn't you, who else could it be?"

"But you acted in self-defense," said Spencer. "Why didn't you tell the truth about what happened?"

"I know I should have, but I just couldn't," she said with a look of embarrassment.

"Oh, now I see," said Spencer. "You were still mad because I turned you down, weren't you?"

Jessie's face turned to stone. "I couldn't believe you'd turn down a chance to have sex with me."

"So you stabbed Porter and blamed me for it just because I wouldn't have sex with you," said Spencer. "Is that about the way it happened?"

"Hey, the lesson here is never scorn a woman."

"Mrs. Harlan, there are people in this town who want me dead. Now you have to make things right. You can't just stand by while they put me to death."

"I can't change my story now," she said. "What would people think of me? No one would ever believe a thing I would say."

"Mrs. Harlan, you can't do this to me."

Jessie turned to walk away. "Next time, don't piss me off," she said and walked out of the room.

Tilly picked up the overflowing laundry basket and stepped out the backdoor to hang them on the clothesline. Seemed like her life was an unending basket of laundry, of dirty dishes and windows that needed to be washed. She was grateful though. She had a job and a nice place to raise her daughter. Most of that she owed to her boss, Mr. Benson. If it hadn't been for him, she wasn't quite sure what she would have done.

"Mama, I need to go see Spencer," said Skeeter as she stopped behind her mother.

Tilly draped a tee shirt over the line and stuck clothespins to hold it in place. "What did you say?"

"I need to go see Spencer."

"You really like that boy, don't you?"

"Outside of Mr. Benson, he's the kindest most wonderful man in the world."

"Land sakes, girl! What did you two do on that date of yours?"

"We talked," said Skeeter. "That's all we did is talk. He's not like other boys, mama. He's sensitive and kind. He has the most wonderful sense of humor."

"But he's in jail, honey," said Tilly picking up another garment. "He's in jail for murder."

"He didn't do it, mama. There's no way he could have. He's too kind and gentle. I was with him that night. It was our first date. He was so happy. He couldn't have done something as horrible as murdering a man, even if it was Mr. Harlan."

"Either way, you got no business inside a jail. You're much too young. Holy Moly, what if something should happen? What if some crazy man were to break out of his cell?"

"Mama, there are only two men in there and they are Sheriff Hicks and Spencer."

"Ain't no crazy men in there?"

"No, mama."

"Well, I don't know," said Tilly hanging the last piece of laundry.

"I'll be real careful, mama. I really will."

"Okay, honey, but if Sheriff Hicks ain't there or he says you can't see that boy, then you get yourself back home here."

Skeeter shot her mother a big smile. "Thanks, mama. I'll be right back."

The jail was on the other side of the downtown district, which was only a ten-minute walk for a young and excited girl like Skeeter. To save time she cut down an alley that would take her past the backdoors of the various downtown businesses and the jail as well. It wasn't the first time she had walked that alley even though her mother had warned her never to go that way. Skeeter never really understood her mother's admonishment. All she really cared about was getting to the jail as fast as she could.

Just as she reached the back of Bailey's Hardware, two men stepped in her way. She jolted to a stop.

"You're Tilly's girl, ain't'cha?" asked one of the men.

"Yes, sir," she replied.

"Where you headed?"

"I don't think that's any of your business."

"Don't get snippy, little girl. You're going to see that boy in jail, aren't you?"

She started to go around them. "Once again, it's none of your business."

One of the men grabbed her shoulder. "Stay away from him, or you'll get hurt."

Skeeter glanced at the man's hand still clinging to her shoulder. "Do you know what they do to men who rape a young girl like me even if I am black?"

"We ain't raping you," he said.

"That's your story," she said with a sly grin. "If you don't remove that hand I'll scream so loud they'll hear me in the next county."

The big man slowly pulled away his hand. "Remember what I said. It's for your own good."

Skeeter walked away in a whimsical, almost defiant gait. She then rounded the corner of the jail and entered the front door.

"Let me guess," said Calvin. "You want to see my prisoner."

"Yes, sir," she said.

"Good Lord, that boy gets more visitors than the pope."

"I just have to see him."

"Go on home, Skeeter," said Calvin. "Your mother would kill be if she knew that I let you in there."

"She already gave me permission."

"She did, huh?"

"Yes, sir."

"You know I should pat you down, but your mother would kill me for that."

"Yes, sir."

"Promise you aren't smuggling in any hacksaws or weapons?"

"I promise."

Calvin pointed at the backdoor. "You've got fifteen minutes."

"Thank you, sheriff," she said and ran to the backdoor.

She excitedly opened the door. Spencer was lying on the bed with his back to her. He turned his head over his shoulder to see who had entered the room.

"Skeeter," he said with a smile spreading across his face. "What are you doing here? It's not safe for you to come here."

"I don't care. I had to see you."

"It's so nice to see you too."

"How have you been? Have they been treating you okay?"

"Oh, I'm fine. The sheriff is real nice to me."

Skeeter's face took on a solemn look. "I know in my heart that you didn't kill anyone, so just tell me who did kill Porter Harlan?"

"I know you won't believe this, but it was Mrs. Harlan."

"How do you know? Did you see her do it?"

"I was asleep when she did it."

"Then how do you know that she did it?"

"She told me."

"She told you?"

"In no uncertain terms."

"Well, what are you going to do?"

"What can I do?"

"Tell someone."

"Do you seriously think anybody in this town would believe me over a Harlan?"

"Is there anything I can do?"

"Yeah, you can pray she confesses."

"It just doesn't seem fair," she said her head bowed.

"It' will all work out," said Spencer.

"How can you say that? Look where you are. You're in jail for what some white woman did and soon to be tried by a bunch of white people."

"I know it doesn't sound promising, but I can't let it get me down."

"You're incredible," she said. "How can you be so optimistic under the circumstances?"

"I've always put myself in God's hands," said Spencer with a gentle voice. "I take care of the small stuff, and I leave everything else up to Him."

Skeeter smiled. "So what you're saying is that we will someday have another date?"

"I guarantee it."

"I'm holding you to that."

"I never break a promise."

"Dinner at the diner again?"

"Maybe even a movie this time."

"It's a date," she said. Her smile disappeared as she grabbed one of the cell bars. Spencer slowly covered her hand with his. She turned hers over and squeezed his.

"Take care of yourself," she said forcing a smile.

"You do the same," he said.

Sheriff Calvin Hicks pushed back from his desk and got to his feet. It was nearly ten o'clock, and he was tired. Bert was due to arrive any minute, so Calvin started for the door. He had just grabbed the doorknob when the phone rang.

Calvin picked up the phone. "Sheriff's office," he said.

"Calvin?"

"Yeah."

"This is Ned Ballows."

"Jesus, Ned, what do you want? I'm on my way to bed."

"Some kid stopped by the house to tell me there's been an accident over on Dry Lane Road. Wanted me to call someone. Said it's pretty bad."

"Shit, Ned. Can't you check it out for me?"

"I can't. Watchin' my granddaughter."

"This better be on the level, or I'm locking your ass up."

"Hey, I'm just telling you what the kid said. You do what you want."

"Who was the kid?"

"Never seen him before."

"God, this stinks."

"What d'ya mean?"

"It sounds like a prank. God damn kids think it's funny to pull shit like this."

"Yeah, but what if it's real?"

"Ned, you're a prick."

"Why? What did I do?"

"Five minutes more and I'd have been out of here, and this would have been Bert's problem."

"Hey, you're the one who wanted to be a sheriff."

"Yeah, yeah," said Calvin. "I'll be out there as fast as my old Chevy can go."

"Bye," said Ned.

Just as Calvin hung up the phone, Bert walked through the door.

"There's been an accident out on Dry Lane Road," said Calvin. "You stay awake and keep an eye on things while I check it out."

"What do you mean by that?" Bert asked. "I don't sleep on the job."

"Jesus, Bert. I've thought about putting in a cot for you. I hate seeing you sleeping in that horrible chair."

Bert smiled. "A cot? Really?"

Calvin opened the door and stood in the doorway. "Stay alert. I've got a bad feeling right now. Can't put my finger on it, but I got a real bad feeling."

Bert patted his holstered revolver and sat down at the desk. "Don't you worry about a thing. Ain't nobody gonna mess with the two of us."

"Just stay awake," said Calvin. He slowly shook his head and closed the door behind him.

It was nearly an hour later. Bert was asleep leaning back against the wall in his chair. The front door burst open, and ten men dressed in hooded white sheets swarmed inside. One of the men instantly grabbed Bert's gun before he had a chance to pull it from its holster.

"Give me the keys, Bert," said one of the men with his hand out.

"What keys?" Bert asked.

"You know what keys. The ones to the jail cells."

"Is that you, Earl?" asked Bert.

"Never mind who I am. Where's the keys?"

Bert scanned the room of men dressed in sheets. "You boys had ought to be ashamed of yourselves."

One of the men pointed a shotgun at Bert. "Where are the fucking keys?" he demanded.

Bert leaned forward and opened a desk drawer. He pulled out a ring of keys and tossed them on the desk.

"You ain't getting away with this, Earl," said Bert. "I know it's you, and I also know that's Ned over there and Charlie is right beside you."

"Grab the keys, Bert, and come with me," said one of the men.

Spencer had been awaken by the commotion and was standing near the back of the cell when the door opened. Bert leaned over and rattled the key in the steel door lock. The door swung open, and the men burst into the cell. Two of the men grabbed Spencer by the arms and led him out of the cell.

"Sit down, Bert, and relax. Calvin will be back after awhile."

They closed the door behind them leaving Bert sitting on the bed. As they filed out of the jail, one of the men tossed the keys on the desk.

"Come on, boys. Let's get this over with."

They marched Spencer around the corner of the jail and into the alley. Nearly a block away, they came upon a tree with a branch that jutted across the alley. A rope with a noose tied on one end dangled from the branch.

One of the men turned to Spencer. "What's the matter with you, boy? You should be screaming and carrying on. Anybody else would."

"I've already made my peace with God. What will be will be."

"Well, God ain't gonna have anything to do with the likes of you. He pretty much frowns on colored folk killin' whites."

"I didn't kill Mr. Harlan."

"Well, if you didn't do it, who did?"

"Mrs. Harlan killed him."

"Oh, so, Mrs. Harlan killed her own stepson. Where did you get a notion like that?"

"She told me."

"Mrs. Harlan killed Porter and then told you all about it. Do you expect us to believe that?"

"All I can say is that I am telling you the truth," said Spencer.

"Come on," said one of the men. "Let's get it over with."

The two men led him closer to the rope.

"Please don't do this," said Spencer. "I have done nothing wrong."

"Come on, guys," said one of the men. "We've only got so much time."

Spencer's body began to shake uncontrollably. "At least give me my day in court. I deserve that much."

The men were now huddled around Spencer. They came to a stop seemingly waiting for a decision.

"Come on," said one of the men. "Let's let it go."

For another moment they stood motionless. Then Earl barged through the crowd and grabbed the noose. "That's enough talk. Bring that son-of-a-bitch over here."

With that, Spencer's legs buckled. His body shuddered as the two men dragged him across the loose gravel. They stopped underneath the rope while Earl slipped it around his neck. He cinched it tightly under his chin.

"You're not going to just hoist him up, are you?" asked Charlie.

"Yeah. Why?" asked Earl.

"That's a hell of a way to go," said Ned.

"Yeah. The least we could do is give him a box or something to jump off. Won't suffer so much that way."

The men scanned the area looking for something to stand on.

"The hell with it," said Earl. He pointed at two men. "You boys grab that end of the rope and get this black bastard in the air."

The two men picked up the loose end of the rope. They stared at each other.

"Go on now," said Earl. "This is taking too long."

They pulled on the rope making it tighten around Spencer's neck. He scrambled to his feet to relieve the pressure. The men pulled on the rope until it was taut. Spencer felt the rope dig into his flesh. He stood on his tiptoes. The rope tightened even more. The men grew silent as they watched in horror. Spencer took a deep breath as he feet lifted off the ground.

Then, without warning, the blast of a shotgun echoed against the buildings and down the alley. The men turned to see Frank Harlan standing in the middle of the alley with his shotgun pointing in the air.

"Let that boy down," he said with a commanding voice.

The men froze.

Frank lowered the gun and pointed it at the men. "I said let that boy down and do it now."

The men released the rope, and Spencer fell to the ground. They stared at Spencer for a moment then turned to Frank.

"What are you doing, Frank?"

"I'm stopping you boys from making a big mistake," said Frank raising the barrel of the gun over the men's heads.

"He killed your son," said Earl.

"You don't know that."

"Your own wife saw it happen."

"The boy deserves a fair trial," said Frank. "Hell, he'll be lucky if he even gets that here in this county."

"For Christ sakes, Frank, there's always a chance that Benson will get the boy off or some kind of reduced sentence. You know how it is today with the court system."

"Yeah, Frank. You turn and walk away, and justice will be served right here and now."

"What you boys are doing out here today is called murder. My son was murdered, and that was bad enough. Let's not make things any worse. Take that noose off that boy's neck and take him back to the jail."

No one moved.

"Do it now," said Frank his voice enraged.

Two of the men slowly picked up Spencer and shuffled off towards the jail.

Chapter Eleven

It was late the next morning when an overweight black woman struggled to step up on the porch. Frank Harlan was sitting at the kitchen tale when she gently knocked the door.

"Well, good morning, Tilly," he said opening the screen door.

"Morning, Mr. Harlan," she said wiping her face with a hankie. "May I come in?"

"Certainly," he said. "Would you like some coffee?"

"Goodness gracious, yes," she said.

"Have a seat," he said pointing at one of the kitchen chairs. He then walked over to the stove and poured her a cup.

Tilly laughed aloud.

"What's so funny?"

"I was just thinking. Other than Mr. Benson, I think you're the first man who has ever served me a cup of coffee."

Frank set the cup on the table. "Well, I'm sorry about that. Every woman deserves to be pampered every once in a while."

"I heard that," she said. "Unfortunately, I've had two men in my life, and neither one of them ever poured me a cup of coffee. Fact is, they up and left me the first chance they got."

Frank paused. "Sorry, Tilly."

"Oh, don't pay never mind. Must be something about me. Losing one is bad enough, but losing another tells me something.

Scott Fields

Frank turned and looked out the door. "By the way, how did you get here?"

"I walked."

"You walked all the way from your house?"

"Ain't got no car."

"Good Lord, lady, that's quite a long walk."

"Well, I had to see you about two things," she said sipping her coffee. First off, let me say how sorry I am about your son. Can't even imagine losing a child."

"Thank you, Tilly. That was very kind of you."

"The other reason I walked out here is to thank you for what you did the other night. That boy would surely be dead right now if it hadn't been for you."

"Thanks Tilly," he said. "I had to do the right thing."

"Nobody in this town would have blamed you if you had just looked the other way. After all, it was your boy who was killed."

"I couldn't have lived with myself if I hadn't stopped those boys."

"Raising young 'uns can be a chore sometimes," said Tilly. "Can't say as I ever really knew your Porter. What was he like?"

Frank shook a cigarette from a pack, then looked up. "Do you mind?"

"Not at all," she said.

He lit it and took a deep breath. "Porter wasn't the greatest kid of all time. Sometimes wonder if he didn't get a lot of his stubbornness and ill temper from me. Anyways, This happened years ago, when Porter was only six. I was taking the family out to a restaurant, which didn't happen that often. We must have been celebrating something, because I don't remember taking them out unless there was some special reason.

"Anyways, Porter asked if he could say grace. I said it was all right, and we all bowed our heads. He started off with something like God is good, and God is great. You know how kids are. He then thanked God for the food and said something at the end about thanking Him even more if mom would get them ice cream for dessert.

"Well, everyone laughed, even the people who were sitting nearby. But there was one woman who was sitting next to us, who began to have a hissy. She said that's what's wrong with America today. She was appalled that a kid would ask God for ice cream.

Hearing this woman ranting about his prayer, Porter burst into tears and asked me if he had done anything wrong. He even asked if God was mad at him.

"As I held him and assured him that he had done a terrific job and God was certainly not mad at him, an elderly gentleman approached the table. He winked at my son and said that he happened to know that God thought that was a great prayer. My son perked up and asked him if he was telling the truth. The old man knelt down beside him and looked over at the woman whose remark had started this whole thing. He said to Porter that it was too bad she never asked God for ice cream. A little ice cream is good for the soul sometimes.

"Naturally, I bought my kids ice cream at the end of the meal. My son stared at his for a moment and then did something I will remember the rest of my life. He picked up his sundae, and without a word, walked over and placed it in front of the woman. With a big smile he told her, 'Here, this is for you. Ice cream is good for the soul sometimes, and my soul is good already.' I never forgot that day all those years ago."

"That's a beautiful story," said Tilly. "You must have been really proud of him"

"Now, it's your turn," said Frank. "Tell me about Skeeter."

Tilly sipped her coffee. "And I suppose you want a kid's story."

"Well, it is your turn."

"Okay, you asked for it. I think the first time I realized that she was special was when she was six years old. Her brother needed an operation, and she was the only one whose blood they could use for the transfusion. I remember the doctor asked her himself if she would be willing to do it. He explained the situation to her. He told her that if she allowed them to take her blood and put it into her brother's arm, he would live. She agreed to do it. In fact, I remember her saying that if that's what it took for her brother to live, so be it.

"Well, they hooked her up, and the transfusion took place. As her blood flowed into her brother's veins, you could see him getting better. His color returned, and we just knew he was going to be all right.

"When it was all over and they finished with the transfusion, the doctor came over to check on Skeeter. That's when she asked him the question. She asked him how much longer. Naturally, the doctor was puzzled and asked her to explain what she meant. She told him that she wanted to know how much longer she had to live. You see when she agreed to allow her blood to flow into her brother's arm, she thought her life would go with it. She loved her brother so much she was willing to give her life for him. That's when I realized she was someone special."

"What an incredible story," said Frank. "You have a wonderful daughter there."

Tilly paused. "The sad part of all this is you've lost your son. I'll bet you must miss him a lot."

"Yes...yes, I do."

"Well, I don't know whether that boy did it or not, but thanks to you he will at least get a trial."

"He hasn't been proven guilty in my book."

"Well, I best be going," said Tilly. "Just wanted to say thanks for what you did."

"Let me drive you home," said Frank.

"Oh, good gracious, no."

"It's no bother."

"How would that look for you to be totin' a colored woman around?"

"As far as I'm concerned, it would be like I'm giving a lady a ride."

"Well, that be one nice thing for you to say, but I believe I'll pass. After all, I ain't never had a white man give me a ride. Wouldn't know how to act." She struggled to get to her feet and lumbered across the floor. As she opened the door, she turned to Frank. "I know I ain't got no business asking this, but do you think Spencer did it?"

"Can't really say without knowing the facts," he said. "It's best to leave that up to a jury."

Tilly smiled. "Any other man would have jumped right on the bandwagon to have that boy executed seeing as how he's colored, but not you. You're a good man, Mr. Harlan, a real good man. God has a special place for people like you," she said and walked out the door.

It was mid-afternoon. The sun was unbearably hot. Frank dropped his hammer and stood straight to rest his back. He had been working hard to finish the repairs to the barn since the tornado. He pulled off his hat and wiped the sweat from his forehead. He had made much progress, but there was much to be done. Frank glanced at the rocking chair on the front porch and decided that it would all wait until he took a break.

Frank sighed as he eased himself into the rocking chair. He pulled his handkerchief from his back pocket and wiped the sweat from his face and neck. The heat was relentless dropping only a few degrees overnight then soaring to nearly triple digits the next day.

Just as Frank closed his eyes to take a nap, the screen door screeched, and Jessie stepped outside. Carrying a large glass of iced-tea, she walked across the porch and took a seat on the steps.

"Got anymore of that iced-tea?" asked Frank.

"Sorry," she said. "This is the last of it."

"Sure am thirsty."

"There's water in the house," she said with a sarcastic tone. "Just turn the little handle, and it comes pouring out."

"Would it be too much to ask for a cold drink?"

"Why? Are your legs broken?"

"You can see me working out here in the hot sun."

Jessie sipped her tea. "Hey, we all got our problems."

"Obviously, I caught you at a bad time," said Frank. "By the way, what have you been doing?"

"Watching my soap."

Frank turned and stared at her with a look of indignation.

"Don't start with me. I've been watching that soap for years, and I'm not stopping now just because you want to work on that silly barn."

Frank turned away. He took deep breaths in an effort to calm his temper. "I want you to stop working at that bar."

"Why?"

"It ain't proper. That's why."

"We need the money."

"We'll be okay."

"We'll be okay? From what little you made at that job? That money will be gone in no time."

"That's not the point," said Frank. "The point is I have no idea what you've been doing while I was gone, but it all ends today."

"What do you mean by that?"

"You know what I mean."

"No, I don't know what you mean."

"I know you've been seeing somebody," said Frank. "I just don't know who it was for sure."

"And I suppose you can prove it," she said. "You wouldn't make such a statement if you couldn't prove it."

"I can't prove it yet, but I will."

"It's downright disgusting that you suspect me of such a thing."

"I went to see Spencer at the jail," said Frank. "Where did you meet this kid?"

"What do you mean by that?"

"Well, you hired him. You must have met him somewhere."

"He came into the bar looking for a job," she said her voice growing louder. "I felt sorry for him. That's all."

"He just wandered into the bar. Is that what you're telling me?"

"The boy sat down, ordered a beer and announced to everyone that he needed a job. It was easy to see that no one was going to help him, so I gave him a job."

"All from the bottom of your heart, I suppose," said Frank with a note of sarcasm.

"As a matter of fact, I…."

"You've never thought of anybody but yourself, and you know it. You're the most selfish person I ever met."

Jessie bristled. "And I suppose you're going to explain to me how giving this guy a job benefited me."

"That's obvious," said Frank. "He's young and good-looking."

"He's also black."

"I know you, Jessie," said Frank. "I know you all too well. You have a hunger for sex that's never satisfied and along comes the forbidden fruit."

"So what you're saying is that I'm a slut."

Frank looked the other way.

"You have the nerve to accuse me of fucking a black man?"

"Actually, I don't think you had sex with him," said Frank turning towards her. "I think he has higher morals than you do. I think you tried, but he wouldn't do it, and that's why I believe you killed my son."

"What did you say?"

"I think you killed my son and blamed it on that boy."

Jessie paused. "Have you gone crazy?"

Frank said nothing.

"Where did you get such a notion?"

Frank remained quiet.

Jessie stared at Frank, until a broad smile appeared on her face. On her knees she crawled across the porch floor until she was next to Frank. "There's no need for us to fight like this," she said turning in his direction. "You know, it's been a long time."

Frank got to his feet. "You're pathetic," he said and marched off the porch.

Nightfall brought peace to the little town of Steam Corners. Everyone brought an end to their daily lives and settled in for a quiet evening and a restful night. Harrison Benson leaned back in his chair and opened his newspaper. It had been a long day, and it felt good to relax. He had nearly drifted off to sleep when Tilly sauntered into the room. She sat on a couch near him and purposely dropped an ashtray to rouse him.

"Sorry," she muttered as he batted his eyes open.

"That's okay," he said sitting straight in his chair. "What can I do for you?"

"Oh, nothing," she said fidgeting with her hands. "Just wanted to check and see if there's anything you needed."

Harrison dropped his paper to his lap. "What's the matter with you?"

"What do you mean?"

"You're one of the loudest, most outspoken women I've ever met, and you're acting like a child on his first day of school."

"It shows?"

"Yes, it shows. Now, what's on your mind?"

"Well, I know you saw that Spencer boy today and was just wondering how it's going?"

"You know you can't ask me questions like that," said Harrison.

"Now you know why I'm acting this way," she said. "I just wanted to know if the boy is going to be okay."

"Why the interest?" he asked. "Is it because of Skeeter?"

"Not entirely, Mr. Benson. I got a feeling about that boy. There ain't no way he went and killed Porter Harlan, and they're fixin' to hang him."

"Well, if he didn't do it, who do you think did?" he asked.

"Oh, I have my suspicions, but that wouldn't be right for me to say."

"Why not?"

"It just ain't right to go around accusing people of things without any proof. They call it gossip, and it just ain't right."

"It's very honorable for you to think that way," said Harrison.

"Well, what's right is right, I always say."

Harrison leaned forward to speak when suddenly a rock crashed through the front window. He instinctively fell to the floor. Tilly nonchalantly leaned over and picked up the rock.

"There's a knot tied to this rock," she said handing it to him. "You might just want to see what it says, even though I can guess what it's all about."

Harrison took the rock as he slipped back into his chair. He cautiously opened the note and read aloud, "Either the nigger dies, or you do." He glanced at Tilly. She had a look of shock on her face.

"Lordy, Mr. Benson, you best be careful now. You know the men around these parts as well as I do, and when they say they gonna do something like that, they pretty much mean it."

"It's so hard to believe…." he muttered.

"What's so hard to believe?" she asked.

"The good people of Steam Corners would be like this."

"Oh, Mr. Benson, you can't blame all the people for this. This is the work of some misguided individual."

"Doesn't it make you mad?" he asked. "Racists who hate you for your color did this."

"You gots to remember that most people are good. We need to learn to appreciate the good people and forgive the bad."

Harrison slowly shook his head.

"And if we can't forgive the bad, we must kick their butts.

Chapter Twelve

The hot summer days finally cooled with the approaching autumn season. There were several days that brought rainfall, but it was only enough to dampen the ground.

The fall also brought the trial of the century for Jefferson County and surrounding areas. It was front page news for that part of the state and beyond. The state was about to try a black man from Detroit for the murder of Porter Harlan, son of a prominent citizen of the county. From the outset, it appeared to be an open-and-shut case. With Jessie Harlan claiming to be an eyewitness, there was not much doubt in anybody's mind as to his guilt. It was simply a matter of going though the motions. As soon as he had been given a fair trial, he would be put to death, and justice will have been served. The only unknown was Harrison Benson and how convincing he could be to the jury.

The jury selection was quick and easy. As everyone predicted, twelve white men were chosen. Harrison protested the appointment of nearly everyone but to no avail. It was if the trial was prearranged to be swift and the results would pronounce the defendant as guilty.

Harrison climbed the courthouse steps amid the sneers and dirty looks of the town folks standing by. The courtroom was filled to capacity with people leaning against the interior walls. The room grew quiet as all eyes followed Harrison as he made his way to a chair next to his client.

"Man, am I glad to see you," said Spencer with a smile.

"Why? Did you think I ducked out on you?" asked Harrison.

"Can't say as I would blame you," said Spencer. "I may not be the smartest guy in the world, but this looks a lot like a modern day lynching."

"Sounds as if you've lost confidence in your attorney."

"Sorry, Mr. Harrison," said Spencer. "It's just I ain't never seen so many white people with blood in their eyes. I swear they look like they're about to take me out back and string me up."

"Well, don't forget here in America everybody is entitled to a fair trial," said Harrison.

"Oh, I haven't forgotten," said Spencer. "Just so those twelve white men on the jury remember."

Harrison glanced at the front of the room. An older man with white hair and a kind face sat at the judge's bench. "Well, at least you got a fair judge."

Spencer looked up as well. "Who is he?"

"His name is Judge Clarence Monk," said Harrison. "He's probably the most liberal and fair-minded judge in the county. Hell, he's even a civil rights activist."

"What's that mean?"

"It means he works hard for black people to have the same rights as whites."

"I thought we already did," said Spencer with a grin. "After all, ain't there some mention in the constitution about all men being created equal?"

Harrison ignored Spencer's question and turned to the man seated at a desk on the other side of the room. He was a middle-aged man neatly dressed with a stern look on his face. "There's your problem, and his name is Sam Wilton."

"Who's he?"

"He's the prosecuting attorney, and he's the best."

"What does he do?"

"You never heard of a prosecuting attorney?"

"No, sir. Ain't never been in court before."

"Well, with any luck, you won't ever be back."

The judge banged his gavel on the table and called the court to order. The murmuring and idle talk came to an abrupt end putting the courtroom into complete silence. He then asked for opening statements, and Spencer watched as Wilton stood and turned to the jury members. He smiled confidently as he made eye contact with each member. It was a polite gesture designed to win favor. He likened it to a personal handshake.

"Your honor and esteemed members of the jury," said Wilton proudly strutting across the courtroom floor. "What we have here is a classic open and shut case. We have a victim, his stepmother who witnessed the murder and the accused all in a neat little package. We will prove beyond a shadow of doubt that the defendant did, in fact, murder Mr. Porter Harlan through the testimony of only three witnesses. I can't speak for Mr. Benson over there, but as for the prosecution we will have you out of there and back home before you can say guilty as charged." He beamed a broad smile at the jury then returned to his seat.

Spencer turned to Harrison. "Begging your pardon, Mr. Benson, but is he for real?"

"He's got a ninety per cent kill rate," said Harrison.

"What does that mean?"

"He gets a conviction on nine out of every ten of his cases."

"And he's the one who is going to try and get me convicted?"

"The one and only," said Harrison.

"Damn," said Spencer. "I'm in trouble."

Harrison smiled as he got to his feet. "Your honor and members of the jury, I cannot make any promises to you as my colleague did. In fact, I had no idea that we were in any kind of hurry here. I was under the impression that we were all gathered here to learn the truth about what happened to Porter Harlan that hot, steamy night. The plain and simple truth is my client had nothing to do with his murder. I will prove to your satisfaction that my client, Spencer Deacon, is completely innocent of the crime." He began to sit down then stopped halfway. "We might not be finished in one day as the prosecution is planning, but when we're done, you'll all agree that my client is innocent."

The trial proceeded just as Sam Wilton had promised. His three witnesses testified and his case against the defendant was completed by the end of the day. It had been quick, but no one was surprised. Everyone had expected the trial to be a matter of routine. After all, nobody was about to allow an outsider especially a black man to come into town, murder a resident and get away with it. Justice had to be served, and it had to be served right away.

It was nearly nine o'clock the next morning when Harrison got out of his car in front of the courthouse. With briefcase in hand, he started up the steps when from out of nowhere Earl Steelman crossed his path and stopped in front of him.

Harrison came to a stop. "Earl, what can I do for you?" he asked with an expressionless face.

"I'm gonna make this fast, counselor," said Earl. "If you ever want to do business in these parts again, you'd better be sure the boy is guilty."

"Are you threatening me, Earl?"

"Call it what you will, but that nigger needs to die."

"What you're doing here is illegal, Earl. You could go to jail for what you just told me."

"Prove I said it," said Earl with an evil grin.

"What?"

"It's your word against mine," said Earl walking away. "Just remember what I said."

The courtroom was buzzing with low murmurs and quiet talk. Harrison took his seat next to Spencer.

"How are you doing, Spencer?" he asked.

"Don't mind telling you that I've been better."

"What's wrong?"

"Unless you got some miracle up your sleeve, I'd say after yesterday, I'm a goner."

Harrison forced a smile. "Don't let that worry you. That was the prosecution's best shot, and it's my turn now."

"Well, I don't know much about law, but that sure enough appeared to me as a pretty good shot."

"Just relax," said Harrison. "The good news is that the defense always goes after the prosecutor. I'll make them forget everything he said."

Spencer paused then leaned closer to Harrison. "Is it true they still hang folks in this state?"

Harrison stopped sorting papers and turned to Spencer. "I don't think you want to talk about this."

"Oh, yes, I do. I really need to know how I'm going to die."

"Why?"

"Well, I think I got a right to know. Besides, I can't believe they still hang people. That seems so barbaric and inhumane."

"Actually, the state electrocutes criminals in the electric chair these days. They say it's more humane, but in reality it isn't. The process takes several minutes while a hanging is instantaneous death."

"It is?"

"There are two ways of hanging a man," said Harrison. "You can put the noose around his neck and hoist him in the air. Doing it that way chokes him and he dies a slow death. The state has you drop four feet which breaks the neck and kills him right there on the spot."

Spencer leaned back away from Harrison. "You're right. We don't need to be talking about this."

The judge took his seat and brought the court to order.

Harrison called his first witness, Calvin Hicks. He ambled across the floor and took a seat in the witness chair. Harrison waited until he was sworn in then slowly walked over to Calvin.

"Marshall Hicks, do you mind if I call you Calvin?"

"I don't know why not," said Calvin. "You've been calling me that ever since you used to play in my kids' sandbox."

There was a low murmur of laughter throughout the courtroom.

"On the night Porter Harlan was killed, you were called out to the Harlan farm. Is that right?"

"Yes, sir," said Calvin. "Mrs. Harlan called me."

"Well, let me ask you something," said Harrison. "Did she seem distressed or upset in any way?"

"No, sir. Not at all."

"When you arrived there, was she crying or hysterical?"

"No, sir."

"How would you describe her emotional state at the time?"

"She was calm and quite helpful."

Harrison paced slowly back and forth. "Under the circumstances, don't you find that a bit odd? I mean, after all, her stepson had just been killed."

Sam Wilton jumped to his feet. "Objection, your honor. That question calls for…"

"I'm going to allow the question," said the judge.

"I guess if you knew Jessie and how she got along with Porter, it really wouldn't be a shock," said Calvin.

"Are you saying Mrs. Harlan and her stepson, Porter, didn't get along?" asked Harrison.

The prosecutor jumped to his feet again. "Your honor, Mrs. Harlan isn't on trial here. Would counselor for the defense please explain where he's going with this line of questioning?"

Harrison stepped over to the judge's bench. "Your honor, the defendant is on trial for murder. His very life depends on our understanding the events that occurred that night."

Judge Monk paused then said, "Continue with your line of questioning."

Harrison turned to Calvin. "Tell me, Calvin. How did they get along?"

"I never heard a nice word that either one said about the other."

"Did you ever see them fighting?"

"Oh, yes," said Calvin. "All the time."

"So, you would characterize their relationship as strained at best," said Harrison.

"That would be a fair description."

"So, when you showed up that night and found Porter dead on the floor, you also found Mrs. Harlan passively sitting nearby and politely answering your questions. Is that about how it was?"

"Tell me, Calvin," said Harrison. "Where was Spencer while this was going on?"

"Spencer was out in the bunkhouse sound asleep."

"Now, think carefully, Calvin. Was he truly asleep, or was he simply laying in bed?"

"Oh, he was asleep, alright," said Calvin. "As a matter of fact, it took me a while just to wake him up."

"Let me get this straight. He took a knife and plunged it deep into Porter Harlan's body, then within minutes went to bed and fell asleep. Is it me, or does this sound a bit bizarre?"

"Sure does to me," said Calvin.

"Let me ask you another question, Calvin," said Harrison. "There must have been blood everywhere."

"Oh, yes, sir. It was a mess alright."

"On the floor, cabinets, tables and such."

"Yes, sir."

"And I suppose there was even blood on Mrs. Harlan."

"Yes, sir. As I recall there was blood on her legs, and some on her shorts."

"Now think carefully, Calvin," said Harrison leaning closer to the stand. "Did it look like the blood had shot on her or did it look as if she had brushed up against some blood? In other words, did it look like it had been smeared?"

"Oh, it wasn't smeared. I can tell you that much. In fact, it looked as if it shot out of Porter and onto Mrs. Harlan."

"So when you went out to the bunkhouse to see Mr. Deacon, did you notice any blood on him?"

"Not a drop," said Calvin.

"Did you see any clothes lying around with blood on them?"

"No, sir."

"Well, tell me this, Marshal Hicks, was this a part of your investigation?"

"What do you mean?"

"Was part of the reason for your going out to the bunkhouse to check for blood?"

"Yes, sir," said Calvin. "I even checked the bottom of his shoes. There was no blood on him nor the bunkhouse."

Harrison paused as he slowly paced the floor then returned to the witness stand. "Marshal Hicks, shortly after arriving onto the crime scene, you purposely examined the garden hose that is just outside the house. Would you mind telling the court why you did such an odd thing?"

"Mrs. Harlan had told me that the defendant had rinsed the blood off by using the hose."

"Did she say how long after he allegedly murdered Porter did he use the hose to rinse off?"

"Yes, sir," said Calvin. "She said it was only minutes afterwards."

"And did you find anything that would clearly prove or disprove her statement?"

"I found blood that had been diluted by water, but I also found chips of dried blood on the ground."

"I don't understand," said Harrison. "How would that be significant? Certainly by the time you had arrived most all of the blood would have been dried."

Calvin shifted his weight as if he were ready to score a right cross. "Certainly the blood that dripped on the ground that wasn't wet would have dried, but it would have stuck to the surface. These chips of blood had dried on another surface like an arm or a leg and then were brushed off onto the ground. In other words, they weren't stuck to anything."

"So, what you're saying is that the person who rinsed off with that hose waited longer than a few minutes after killing Porter, possibly a half-hour."

"That would be my guess," said Calvin.

Harrison turned and started for his seat. He then stopped and turned to Calvin. "When you entered the bunkhouse and awoke Mr. Deacon, what was his reaction?"

"He looked a bit confused even frightened."

"Did he have any idea why you were there?"

Wilton jumped to his feet. "Objection," he shouted.

"Over ruled," said the judge. "You may answer the question."

All eyes turned to Calvin. "He looked as if he didn't have a clue."

"Your witness," said Harrison returning to his seat.

"Marshal Hicks," said Wilton getting to his feet. "You say that Mr. Deacon was asleep and didn't have a clue as to what was going on."

"Yes, sir."

"When you think about it, what are the chances that a black man could hide around here?" asked Wilton. "I mean, after all, there aren't too many places that he wouldn't stand out from the crowd."

"I guess I don't understand…"

"Well, the best thing he could do is nothing. If he takes off running from the scene, he looks guilty. If he just simply goes off to bed, who would suspect him of such a crime?"

Calvin said nothing.

"And you say he had no blood on his clothes," said Wilton turning to the jury. "Isn't it quite possible that he changed what he was wearing and possibly destroyed the bloodied clothes?"

Calvin sighed and leaned back in his chair. "Yes, that's possible."

"That's all, your honor," said Wilton returning to his seat.

"You're excused," said the judge turning to Calvin. "Call your next witness."

Harrison slowly got to his feet. "Mrs. Jessie Harlan," he announced.

Jessie got to her feet and walked across the floor. She was wearing a tight red dress with the hem halfway up her legs. All eyes followed her as she sat in the chair and crossed her legs. She smiled as she spread one leg wide then lifted it over the other. Everyone in the courtroom froze as they watched the hem of her dress settle just below her waist.

"Now, Mrs. Harlan…"

"Jessie," she blurted.

"Excuse me," said Harrison.

"Jessie. Call me Jessie. I like people thinking of me as a Jessie rather than a Mrs. Harlan."

"Okay, Jessie," said Harrison with a smile. "Now, we all know there were only three people at your house that night. One of them is dead, and another is on trial. That leaves you. I guess we could call you a witness. Let me ask you a question, Jessie. Were you drinking that night?"

"I guess I don't remember."

"That's funny. Marshal Hicks said he found six empty beer bottles in the yard."

"Maybe, the boy drank them," she said pointing at Spencer.

"I thought he was on a date. Could it be that you drank them?"

Jessie paused. "I guess that's possible."

"Were you intoxicated?"

"Oh, no."

"Six bottles of beer, and you weren't drunk?"

"I hold my liquor pretty darn well," she said with a laugh.

"Still, Jessie, six bottles of beer is a bit much. Would you say that you had even a slight buzz?"

"Oh, I suppose you could say that."

"During the investigation, you told Marshal Hicks that the defendant came home from a date and was quite angry. Is that correct?"

"Yes."

"Did he say why he was angry?"

"He said something about not getting any from his date with Skeeter."

"When you say any. I'm assuming you mean sex."

"Yeah...sure."

"Now, you're saying he came up to the house. I thought he lived in the bunkhouse. Why would he come to the house at that late hour?"

"He'd been drinking. I could tell right away. He was ranting on about that little bitch not giving it up for him."

"You know, Jessie," said Harrison. "You can go to jail for perjury."

"Oh, no. I ain't lying," said Jessie. "I'm telling the truth. The man was out of his head. When he finally settled down and took a deep breath, he started after me. It was horrible. He tore my shirt off right there in front of God and everything. I was never so humiliated in my life. I mean after all I'm standing in front of a black boy with no top on. I think we all know that ain't right. It just ain't right for no colored boy to see a white woman like that. Then it happened. I knew that once he got his eyes full, he would want more. He started to touch my breasts. At first, he just lightly touched them almost like he was afraid of them or something. Then before I knew it, he was squeezing them. Sqeezin' them 'til it hurt. I wanted to scream, but I knew, damn well, it would do no good. Ain't nobody around them parts for miles. I ain't been the same since that night. Can't never get it out of my head. Imagine some black boy a lookin' at a white woman's breasts and a touchin' them as well. Time was they'd have strung him up by the neck for doin' something like that. Sure enough. Ain't no doubt about it. As I was saying, the next thing I know he's a kissing and licking them. I kinda knew where this was leading and sure enough he orders me to take off my shorts. I tell me no, and before I knew it he had picked up a butcher knife and told me either I take them off or he's cutting them off. In his condition, there was no way I was going to let him stick a knife down there, so I started to unbutton my shorts. I went as slow as I could seeing as how I had nothing on under them. I had just started to slide them down to the floor when Porter came in. I gotta tell you I was never so glad to see anybody as I was to see him walking through that door. He took one look at what was going on and lunged at Spencer. Hell, I never saw the knife go in. Next thing I know there's blood everywhere and Porter falling to the floor. And that's how it happened. I don't care what anybody else says.

Harrison slowly shook his head then smiled. "This is quite a story you have here, Jessie. Quite a story indeed. You were even clever enough to stir up primal feelings with the story about the defendant's sexual advances. You are a smart lady. Much smarter than you let on." Harrison then leaned forward his head near Jessie's. "Now let's talk about what really happened. Mr. Deacon came home that night not in a bad, rather in a state of pure happiness from his date with Skeeter. He didn't come to the house, rather you came out to the bunkhouse, and when he wouldn't give into your sexual advances, you got mad and stormed off. Shortly after that, Porter comes home completely intoxicated. He comes after you, and you stick him with a butcher knife. You could have admitted to it, and it would have been called self-defense, but you were still mad at Mr. Deacon.

Blaming him for the crime was the perfect one-two punch. You get rid of Porter and get back at Mr. Deacon. Isn't that the way it happened, Jessie Harlan?"

By that time, the prosecutor had been on his feet and nearly hoarse from screaming, "Objection." The judge strongly admonished Harrison for such an outbreak. Legally, it served no purpose, but in reality he sent a clear message to the jury.

The trial wasn't finished in one day like Prosecutor Sam Wilton had hoped for, but it didn't take any longer than three days either. A parade of witnesses took the stand, and in no time all of the town folks of Steam Corners had formed an opinion.

The jury was led out of the courtroom and into a small windowless room near the back of the courthouse. There was a long table with twelve chairs. They were instructed to sit down and collectively arrive at a verdict.

Spencer was led a to a holding cell to wait for the jury's decision. He was there for only a few moments when the door swung open. He looked up to find Calvin standing next to Skeeter.

"Oh, my God," said Spencer getting to his feet.

"I'd get fired if anybody found out I done this," said Calvin. "I can only give you kids a few minutes," he said and walked out of the room.

"How are you," said Skeeter reaching one hand through the bars.

Spencer took her hand and held it firmly in his. "I'm doing okay."

Skeeter's face turned solemn. "I've been watching your trial."

"Doesn't look too good, does it?"

"I thought Mr. Benson did a good job, didn't you?" she asked.

"Oh, yes. I think he did just fine."

"I sit there staring at that Mrs. Harlan, and I can't believe she would let this get this far," she said with a touch of anger in her voice. "She sits there with that smug look on her face and bobbing that leg back and forth. What I wouldn't do to her if I could get the chance."

"Let's just hope the jury isn't fooled by her," said Spencer.

"I hope so, Spencer," she said. "I really do, but I'm scared, really scared. After all, when it comes right down to it, it's your word against a Harlan."

"Yeah, and she's white and I'm not.

"Is there anything I can do?"

"Keep your fingers crossed."

Skeeter paused as she thought about what she was about to say. "Spencer, when this is over, let's you and me run as far away from this town as we can get."

"You want to run away with me?" asked Spencer with a stunned look. "You hardly know me."

"That doesn't matter," she said. "We got nothing holding us here but bad memories."

"What about your mother?"

"She'll understand."

Spencer slowly shook his head. "You want to run away with a man on trial for murder?"

"A girl has to trust what's in her heart. I know you didn't do anything wrong, and my heart tells me that I love you."

Spencer smiled. "Are you sure about this?"

"I've never been more sure of anything in my life."

Spencer was about to speak when the door opened. "The jury is returning to the courtroom," said Calvin. "Let's get on in there."

Skeeter made her way to the back of the courtroom and upstairs to the balcony, while Calvin led Spencer back to his seat. A hush fell on the courtroom as the jury members filed in. In spite of the fact that most everybody was reasonably certain that the verdict would be guilty, there was a great deal of tension in the air. Many had doubts as to his guilt but greatly feared being accused of being a "nigger-lover", so they kept their beliefs to themselves. Many just wanted this outsider to be taken away, and maybe things could return to normal. After all, Steam Corners never had a murder until this boy from Detroit showed up. One thing was for certain, this outsider didn't belong in these parts and needed to go away.

The judge called the court to order and asked the jury if they had arrived at a verdict. An older man dressed in a suit stood and said, "We have, your honor."

"How do you find the defendant?" asked the judge. "Guilty or not guilty?"

An eerie stillness fell on the room as the man opened a small scrap of paper. "We find the defendant, Spencer Deacon, guilty of murder in the first degree."

The room erupted in loud, disruptive talk. News reporters ran from the room to get to a telephone while the judge tried to restore order. Spencer leaned back in his chair as he tried to assimilate what had just happened. He turned his head and found Jessie staring at him. She was biting her fingernails and bobbing one leg. He looked to see any remorse on her face and found none.

Chapter Thirteen

Days spilled into weeks, until it was finally the day before Spencer was to be transferred to the state penitentiary to wait for his day of execution. He was sitting on the side of his cot when the door opened, and Calvin walked in with Skeeter at his side.

"Skeeter," shouted Spencer as he rushed to her.

"Hi, Spencer," she said thrusting her hands through the bars.

"What are you doing here?" he asked.

"I had to see you one more time before they...before they took you away."

"I'm so glad you did. I was hoping I'd get to see you again."

"Doing okay?"

"For the most part."

"We need to make plans," she said with a smile.

"Plans?"

"We talked about running away. We didn't even talk about where we're going to live."

"Huh?"

"I was thinking that Springfield would be a nice town to live in. What do you think?"

Spencer's smile disappeared. "Skeeter, I'm not getting out of here."

"Yes, you are."

"Later today, they are taking me to the state pen."

"You've got to think positive."

"Well, I'm afraid it's going to take more than that."

Skeeter's face sobered as well. "There's got to be something we can do."

"The only chance I got is for Mrs. Harlan to tell the truth, and that ain't gonna happen."

"That's it!" said Skeeter turning to leave. "That's how I can get you out of here."

"What are you going to do?" asked Spencer.

"I'm going to go see Mrs. Harlan and convince her to tell the truth."

"No, Skeeter," said Spencer. "You stay away from her. She's a very dangerous woman."

She opened the door and looked at Spencer over her shoulder. "Don't worry about a thing," she said and walked out.

***

Jessie poured herself a tall glass of iced tea and stepped out onto the porch. It had been a long, hot summer, and the crisp autumn air felt good on her skin. She sat on the porch swing and kicked the floor to put it in motion. She sipped her tea and stared across the decaying farm. The outbuildings were all but piles of rotting lumber, and weeds grew now where once there were none. Seemed like such a shame when you considered what it once was. She smiled as she remembered better days. It seemed as if the Harlans could do no wrong. They had the biggest and best farm in the county maybe even the state. Farm hands by the dozens living out there in the bunkhouse. Those were the days, all right. The outbuildings were pristine standing tall with bright white paint against lush green grass. Hard working men and hot summer days with soft, cool evenings for relaxing. It was a grander time then, a time seemingly lost forever, stolen by the endless draught and the relentless summer heat.

Jessie jumped from her dream-like state as she heard approaching footsteps. She turned to see Skeeter standing beside the porch.

"Good morning, Mrs. Harlan," she said a little out of breath.

Jessie sipped her tea. "Well, ain't this a surprise? What the hell do you want?"

"Where is Mr. Harlan?"

"He's still in bed. Now, what do you want?"

"I want to talk to you."

"You walked all the way out here?"

"Yes, ma'am."

"Well, you just wasted your time, little girl. I got nothing to say to you."

"Why? Is it because I'm black?"

"Mostly the company you keep."

"They're going to execute him," said Skeeter. "You know that, don't you?"

"That's generally what happens to murderers."

"He didn't murder Porter, and you know it."

"The court says he did."

"How could you do this?"

"Do what?"

"You're going to stand by and let them execute an innocent young man when you know the truth."

Jessie leaned forward. "And just what is the truth?"

"You killed Porter, and you pinned it on Spencer."

Jessie leaned back and stared at a squirrel as it circled an old bird feeder searching for food. "Where have you been, Mr. Squirrel? Ain't been no food in there in years."

"Mrs. Harlan, talk to me," said Skeeter.

Jessie watched as the squirrel gave up and ran away. "That's right. Ain't nothing worth nothing on this farm. Run away. Run far away from this farm. Ain't nothing left here."

"Mrs. Harlan, please talk to me."

Jessie's face had turned cold. She stared as if she were in a trance. "I married him for his money, you know. Not many women will admit to that. It's pretty obvious, don't you think? Look at him. He's old and never was very handsome. All he ever had going for him was this ranch and the money his pappy left him. Why else would someone like me marry a man like him? I suppose in a way we loved each other at one time. It wasn't always like this. There were better times, times of cut roses wrapped in green paper and of soft, linen dresses. People made way for the Harlans back then. They even whispered to each other about them rich Harlans and how lucky we were. Yeah, those were the days, all right.

"He wasn't mine, you know. Porter. He came as a package deal. Never did like him. We never got along. All he ever wanted was to have sex with me. Don't know why I never did it. Hell, it's not like he was family, and, besides, he had to have been better than his daddy. Oh, I know how that must sound. I suppose it ain't right to talk about screwing your stepson. Well, that's one thing I didn't do. Contrary to popular belief, I do have some standards, some morals. It's not like I didn't think about it from time to time. One of his little conquests told me he was the best. She said he would take care of a woman until she was out of her head. Never could figure how he ever learned that. The way she went on and on about his lovemaking left me dumbfounded. Ain't no way he learned that from his daddy. His daddy was on and off before you ever knew it. Of all the men I've had in my life, I had to go and marry the God-awful worst at sex. I guess there's a price to pay when you marry for money. I guess, in a way, I asked for it. Pretty much knew he wasn't a very sensitive man with a woman's needs in mind. He was a dumb ole dirt farmer, and they're all the same. They work hard and live hard lives. Not much room for a woman other than to cook their meals and wash their socks."

Jessie paused then slowly turned to Skeeter. "He came after me, you know. It was purely self-defense. He came home drunker than I had ever seen him. Then when he saw me without my shirt on, he came after me. I ain't never seen a man who looked like he did. Most men have a smile on their face when they are trying to get you in bed, but not this time. The look on his face chilled me to the bone. Thought for sure he was gonna do something bad to me. Yeah, I killed him. Stuck him with a butcher knife. Went in a lot easier than I imagined. Felt good too. I know how that must sound, but God I hated him.

"I knew at the time I hadn't really done nothing wrong. Like I said, it was self-defense. Don't imagine it would have even gone to trial. I know now that I done wrong blaming your Spencer. Seemed like the thing to do at the time." Jessie smiled. "Damn, he's a good-looking boy. I wanted him so bad. Don't think I ever wanted a man that way. He could have done anything he wanted to me, and I would have loved every minute of it. Seen him without his shirt you know. My God, he was something. There were times I thought I was going to get one just looking at him. I ain't never seen a black man without his clothes on. Would have been something. That's for sure.

"Oh, I tried to get him in bed. That's for sure. Tried everything I knew, but he wouldn't budge. He was some kind of righteous bastard or something. No matter what I did, he wouldn't go to bed with me. I wanted him so bad that night. Damn, I wanted him. I even took off my shirt. Thought that might do it, but he held fast to his morals. I guess that was the last straw. I had had enough. I had been drinking a little and wasn't thinking too clear. Then when he turned me down once again, I guess I just exploded. I got so mad I wanted to kill him. Swear to God. Ain't that a queer thing? Lust after a man and then want to kill him. Anyways, I guess the timing was all wrong. Minutes later, I killed Porter, and it seemed like the thing to do was to pin it on Spencer. Like they say, ain't nothing like the wrath of a scorned woman."

Jessie smiled. "The one thing I've learned in life is that there's a price to be paid for everything. If your Spencer had been a little nicer to me, he wouldn't be paying the price he's paying now."

Just as Jessie leaned back and sipped her tea, the screen door opened. She turned to see Frank standing in the open doorway.

"Why?" he asked with a stern voice. "Why did you do it?"

"How long have you been standing there?"

"I heard enough to drag your ass down to the jail and have you confess."

"They'll throw me in jail for withholding evidence or some such shit."

Frank leaned over until his face was in front of hers. "They're going to execute that boy if you don't confess."

"You'd rather I go to jail than see a nigger get executed?"

"Absolutely," he said taking her by the arm. "Why I married you I will never know, but that's all coming to an end."

Two weeks later, Spencer and Skeeter finished loading the last of the luggage. Skeeter said good bye to her mother and they both got in the car. Spencer put his hand on the key and turned to Skeeter.

"Springfield?"

"Springfield, it is," she replied.

He started the engine, and they drove out of sight.

The End